LAST ROOM
AT THE CLIFF'S EDGE

A DETECTIVE LINDA MYSTERY

MARK MCNEASE

Copyright © 2016 Mark McNease
Published by MadeMark Publishing
New York City
www.MadeMarkPublishing.com

Cover design by MadeMark Media
Cover image licensed from Depositphotos

ISBN 10: 0-9916279-9-7
ISBN 13: 978-0-9916279-9-8

ALSO BY MARK MCNEASE

Listen to the Fear—Audiobooks

Murder at Pride Lodge
Pride and Perilous
Death by Pride
Death in the Headlights
Stop the Car

Kyle Callahan Mysteries

Murder at Pride Lodge
Pride and Perilous
Death in the Headlights
Death by Pride
The Pride Trilogy
Kill Switch

Other Books & Writing

Stop the Car, a Kindle Single
Rough & Tumble: A Dystopian Love Tragedy

Outer Voices Inner Lives (Co-Editor and Publisher, Lambda Literary
Award finalist for anthology, 2014)

In Harmony with the Seasons: Herbs, Nutrition and Well-Being, by
Cathy McNease (Publisher)

ACKNOWLEDGMENTS

I want to thank some fellow writers who keep me in touch with creative urgency and remind me why I sit alone at a computer most mornings: Marshall Thornton, Jon Michaelsen, David Lennon and David Swatling, all fine mystery writers and now, I'm glad to say, friends.

Lee Lynch, whose graciousness is matched only by her talent. And Jean Ryan, among those I consider a wordsmith as well as a writer. They're not always the same.

My husband Frank must always be acknowledged because he lives with the sight of me alone in the pre-dawn darkness, only a desk lamp to illuminate me as I sometimes mumble the sentences my characters are whispering to me. And my copy editor/proofreader Robin Feldman, whose attention to detail sets me free to write without worrying what I'd misspelled or if I'd misspoken.

It appears we don't write alone, after all.

– Mark McNease

DEDICATION

For John F. Higgins

Thanks for reminding me.
Love the pom-poms.

A STORM APPROACHES

CAYLEY DREES was nervous. She hadn't heard from her confidential source for two days and she was supposed to meet him tonight. The timing could not be worse. A storm had made land the past six hours, covering Maine in thickening sheets of rain. She'd not had far to drive, just from Wathingham, where she lived and worked, to the outskirts of Lonesome Pointe, but the driving had been slow and treacherous. Drivers, including herself, had pulled off the highway at intervals to let the rain slow enough for them to see again. Visibility for parts of the 90 minute trip (now closing in on two and a half hours with weather delays) was approximately zero. She was relieved and curious to finally see the fading billboard announcing the Cliff's Edge Motel just two miles up the road. At the rate she was going it would be a long two miles, but she was comforted to know her destination was in sight.

At twenty-three Cayley was already among those young achievers who made names for themselves on "30 Under 30" lists and nods to up-and-comers that appeared annually, praising the next generation's best and brightest. She was going places, and like others of her type, she was the first to declare it. A natural journalist, Cayley had ignored the probability of an internship at the Boston Globe or the Philadelphia Inquirer, choosing instead to learn her reporting chops at little Wathingham, Maine's, All Pointes Bulletin. But she had her reasons: she was a small pond girl at heart, and she intended to be the biggest fish in it. Had she gone with the Globe or the Enquirer she would be covering news that mattered to much of the world, but she would be the fourth journalist down on the left, in a cubicle listening to a hundred other journalists talk to sources and crank out stories with bylines nobody noticed. The ladder they climbed was steeper, and much more crowded. This way she could move back to Wathingham where her family lived and be a star. It would take time to reach the top, but not as much time. The All Pointes had a staff of only seven, including the part-time receptionist. It was a fiefdom she could find herself running in just a few years.

She wasn't happy being assigned the obits, but it was part of the game she had to play. Everyone had to start somewhere, and it was the kind of assignment a new reporter was expected to do. The paper's publisher and editor, a no-nonsense woman named Lucille Proctor, had taken a liking to Cayley when she'd known her casually as a high school student in town and Cayley's journalism class had spent the day shadowing All Pointes reporters. Lucille accepted her internship application the day after it arrived. She could have said yes that same afternoon, but why seem too eager? Few young people as talented and determined as Cayley ever returned, and certainly showed no interest in internships at the All Pointes when they could cover celebrity drug overdoses for the L.A. Times, where it also happened to be warm most of the year.

Cayley had been reporting on dead people for almost a year now. She covered other things, too: local festivals, some interviews, and an occasional movie review for which she was reimbursed the cost of one ticket, a soda and a small popcorn. It was the opposite of glamorous. There was a time during the summer when Cayley questioned her decision to return to Wathingham. She'd posted a dozen death notices, contacted a few next of kin when something they'd submitted was questionably written or, in one case, to determine if the deceased was truly dead, since she swore she'd seen the man in the pharmacy the day before.

And then it happened: the call from her source. He sounded nervous—in fact, he sounded nervous every time she subsequently spoke to him, as if someone might hear them. They never emailed. He insisted all emails were read by the government, or at least by the employers of everyone sending them. He wanted nothing in writing, he said, he just wanted her to know what happened. But first, about that obituary you ran for Russell Drover ...

"Russell Drover?" she'd said, trying to remember which one it was and when it was published. She had been sitting at her desk rewriting copy when the call came in, the last of the day to be transferred by Rudy, the part-time office guy. (Rudy was sweet, distracted and more interested in finding a girlfriend than furthering his career, which was why he was a part-time receptionist at twenty-six.)

"The old guy who owned the Cliff's Edge outside of Lonesome Pointe," the voice said, sounding as if he'd cupped his hand over the phone.

2

"The Cliff's Edge ..."

"Are you a reporter or a parrot?"

She'd almost hung up on him then. She'd been pranked a few times, always by kids who thought annoying strangers on the phone was hysterical. But something in his tone, his nervousness, made her take a deep breath and refrain from snapping.

"I'm a reporter, Mr ...?"

"Never mind that," he'd said. "I just called to tell you that you got it wrong."

"Wrong?" she'd said, immediately regretting repeating him again.

"Yes, wrong."

"How's that?"

She was sitting up now. She'd taken a pencil from an All Pointes coffee cup she used for them and poised it over a thin white reporter's notebook. Something told her this was different, this had substance.

"He didn't shoot himself like they said."

"We didn't say that either, Sir. Suicide never reads well in an obituary."

"You think I'm playing with you, is that what you think?"

His sharpness startled her. She sensed she had to be careful if she wanted him to keep talking.

"Are you telling me he was killed by someone else?" she asked, still not recalling the obituary in question but certain it had said nothing about suicide. Families preferred to say "a sudden illness." It didn't matter now. She was being offered something she knew was bigger than the obituary beat, something people would talk about.

"He was murdered, yes," the man said. This time his tone was flat, almost sad.

She waited a moment, letting him breathe while she decided how best to proceed. "Is there more, Sir? Is there something you'd like to tell me, like ... who you believe killed Mr. Drover?"

"Oh, I know who killed him."

Cayley felt the chill through the phone. *Yes*, she thought, *yes, I'm sure you do know, but will you tell me? Pretty please? Or will this be difficult ...*

"And I know why," he said. "It was because of what happened."

"What happened?"

"Yeah, what happened."

Very carefully now: "When?"

"A long time ago."

He'd hung up on her then. She was remembering it, complete with the sense of frustration it had caused her, as she pulled into the parking lot of the Cliff's Edge. Most of the parking spots were taken and she wondered if the place was not quite the dive she'd read about. It wasn't much to look at, even with rain obscuring her vision through the windshield. One-story, with a long, beige stucco front revealing fewer than a dozen rooms, their windows looking out on the storm, half of them blocked by dark, thick drapes. A child's toy fire truck sat outside one room, and Cayley wondered if it would be rusted by all the water. She flipped up her umbrella, slammed her car door shut and made a dash for the motel's front door.

She glanced briefly at the motel's orange neon "Vacancy" sign, glad now they still had a room or two left. She had not made a reservation. No one knew about the story she was covering or the explosion it would cause once it was published. Her source had insisted on secrecy and anonymity, until tonight. He would reveal himself to her—who he was, what he looked like, and what he'd done. It had all been kept in a blackout, with only the two of them knowing they'd made contact and what he had been telling her. Tonight was a turning point. Tonight her life would change. Until then, nobody knew what she was doing or where she was.

She opened the glass door to the Cliff's Edge office and hurried inside.

* * *

She did not like the way the man at the front desk was looking at her. She'd even considered going somewhere else, but she was supposed to meet her source here in just a few hours, and where would she go, anyway? The storm was only getting worse, and the options for spending the night were few. She would not drive back at this point, not without speaking to her source or confirming he'd gotten cold feet and was not coming.

The desk man—for what else would she call him?—had reacted strangely to her arrival, as if he'd been expecting her. For one thing, when she asked if they had a room available, she could swear he'd said, "Sure thing, we've got your room."

"*My* room?" she'd said.

"*A* room," he said. "I said 'a' room, Miss . . . ?"

"Drees. Cayley Drees."

"That's a pretty name," said the man, who had given his name as Lenny. He smiled at her, a flat, forced expression that did not extend beyond the corners of his mouth. His hair was tied back in a dirty-blond ponytail that looked either gelled or filthy, and his forearms were scarred by dark, overly detailed tattoos she would have to stare at to decipher; she was not about to stare.

"Has anyone called for me?" she asked.

His smile vanished. "Why would they call me?"

"I don't mean you personally. I mean has anyone called the Cliff's Edge looking for me."

"No, no calls for you. Hardly anybody calls here even on a busy day, and we don't have many of those. But maybe with the storm coming we'll get filled up. Kinda looks that way."

"Maybe," Cayley said. She was perplexed that her source had not made contact or called the motel. He'd gone silent the past twenty-four hours and that was troubling. She'd even considered calling off the trip—driving in yet another "storm of the century" was not her idea of enjoyable travel—but this story was important and she wasn't about to let a fading hurricane get in the way. This was the kind of investigative piece Cayley had imagined herself writing all those years she studied journalism. The sort of shocking exposé that would get her boss's notice and, once she had that, the notice of people well outside the little Maine enclaves who read the All Pointes Bulletin. She was too level-headed to fantasize a Pulitzer, but this could be a step on her way to one, something she could look back on as the beginning of big things.

"Is there any place to eat around here?" Cayley asked. "I didn't see anything driving in, and I've never been to Lonesome Pointe before. What kind of name is that, anyway?"

Lenny stared at her a moment. "I'm guessing you're not here to make friends. It was named 'cause it has only one lighthouse, which someone at some point in time thought was lonesome out there all by itself. Get it? It's also three miles north. This is unincorporated territory you're in right now. Not a lighthouse in sight."

"Thanks for letting me know, Mister . . ."

"Winfrow. But you can call me Lenny. No reason not to."

"Lenny. I appreciate the information. It's always good to know when you're in unincorporated territory. Now, is there some place to eat? I'd love to grab something before the storm keeps us in completely."

"There's a diner two miles back, I'm surprised you didn't see it."

"I may have. I was a little distracted."

"That's dangerous."

"Pardon?"

"Distracted driving," said Lenny.

"Right, totally. I drove past the only place to eat and I never saw it!"

Lenny smiled and said, "It's not exactly the only place to eat. I could make you something. Got a nice little room in the back, kitchenette and everything."

Using his thumb, he pointed toward a door behind him, left ajar just enough to see that it led into a back room.

"Old Man Drover—that's who owned this place until his tragic death a few months back—he had it built for himself, so he wouldn't take up one of the motel rooms. Need 'em for pretty ladies like you."

He grinned, sending a shiver through Cayley. She thought he looked like a lizard when he smiled. She expected his tongue to dart across the front desk and lick her cheek. She stepped back.

"Thanks so much for the offer, Lenny, but I couldn't put you out."

"No trouble at all." He seemed to be enjoying her discomfort.

"I'll be back in an hour, I'd guess. If anyone calls ..."

"I'll be sure to take a message," he said, leaning back on his stool.

Lenny put his arms over his head, exposing sweat stains in October. It was an unattractive sight, which Cayley was sure he knew. The front desk clerk at the Cliff's Edge was someone she wished she'd never met and hoped it was a one-time encounter.

"Well, bye, then," Cayley said, dropping the room key in her purse and turning for the door.

"Bye, then," Lenny said. He watched her hurry outside into the growing darkness, then reached for his cell phone. The package had arrived.

TWO FOR THE ROAD

LINDA SIKORSKY wasn't looking forward to the drive to Maine but she would not tell Kirsten. It would take at least six hours, much of that in a storm the weather service had been warning about for the past week. She'd thought of suggesting they postpone the trip, but she knew the price for it would be days of sulking by Kirsten, delivered with a large side order of disappointment. Her wife had been planning this trip for two months, convinced it would be just what she needed to finish her first mystery, whose central character was transparently modeled after Linda. "The Rox Harmony Mysteries" had become Kirsten McClellan's obsession. Linda was so relieved Kirsten had found a calling in retirement, even if writing was an avocation Linda thought put food on very few tables, that she withheld her reservations about a fictional lesbian detective based on her. Nor did she speak to Kirsten of the ego deflation that surely lay ahead in mixed reviews, unpredictable book sales and that small matter of finding a publisher. None of these things were worth causing Kirsten to fret more than she normally did. For Linda, just driving to Maine in terrible weather, after an unexpected delay caused by her mother's emergency in Philadelphia, provided stress enough.

The women lived in a small house in Kingwood Township, New Jersey, that Linda had inherited from her Aunt Celeste. Her mother's only sibling, Celeste had died on the back porch the spring before last, watering the flowers she'd kept for years in plastic beds hung from a wrought-iron railing surrounding the small space. There was just enough room on the porch for a table and four chairs. Linda had spent many Sunday mornings having coffee with her aunt after driving from New Hope, Pennsylvania, across the river into Jersey. She usually visited her mother the day before, making those weekends a sort of twofer: visit Mom one day, Aunt Celeste the next, and promise to be back in two weeks, three tops if something came up to delay her.

That "something" was sometimes homicide. Linda was then on the New Hope Police Force as its only female detective. She'd put in nearly twenty years, the last six in homicide, when Celeste died and left her the perfect place to retire: five acres of wooded land, a mile's drive on 651 from the Delaware River. Timing, as Linda knew, was everything. She'd met Kirsten McClellan that January, inherited the house in September, and married Kirsten the following March. Now they were living very rural lives and slowly but surely adjusting to them.

* * *

At first Kirsten had tried to talk Linda into keeping the house as a second home and moving into Kirsten's New Hope condo instead. Linda had maintained apartments all her adult life and had no particular emotional attachment to any of them. She did, however, have a strong emotional attachment to her aunt's little house in the woods, and she resisted Kirsten's offer to move in with her as lovingly but firmly as possible. They weren't yet married when Linda inherited the house, and she'd worried for a short while if living there would be a deal breaker for Kirsten. There was none of the city glamour (as far as New Hope can be called a city), none of the bustle and glitz out there among the trees and creatures. But Linda loved it. It was that love that swayed Kirsten more than anything. She knew Linda was not the high-end condo type. She also knew they had both reached new chapters in their lives, and that meeting each other was as great a catalyst for change as either would likely ever experience.

Linda left the police force and opened her "vintage everything" store in New Hope just two months later, selling clothes, knick-knacks, prized 1960s TV show lunch boxes, even buttons from political conventions spanning a century. *For Pete's Sake* was named after her father, who'd been killed when Linda was just eight years old and the family lived in Cincinnati. Pete Sikorsky was a cop. He was also the love of Linda's life, which provided her with a decades-long excuse not to love anyone, not to risk the pain and grief of loss, and to essentially stay closeted. (While she believed she had never kept a secret of her sexuality, let alone a *dark secret*, she had recently admitted to herself that a great need for privacy and a fear of intimacy were not the only reasons she'd never come out; self-doubt, uncertainty about the reactions of others, including her mother, and not a tiny bit of internalized homophobia also played their parts.)

Pete Sikorsky went to the local grocery store one Saturday

morning to get Linda's favorite cereal and a carton of milk. They'd run out of both, and while Linda was not the sort of daughter to demand it, her father said it was no problem, he'd go down to the store and be back in ten minutes. He never came home. A police officer for twelve years at the time, a man who'd served as Military Police in Vietnam, a cautious adult and doting father of his only child, Pete did not take his service pistol with him that morning. Would it have mattered? Linda asked herself that for the next forty years, even as she now prized her father's Colt revolver, the one she'd shot so many times at ranges. Would it have mattered if they'd not run out of cereal? Or was life, no matter how much we want to believe otherwise, predetermined to such a fine point that nothing at all could have stopped what happened or changed the course of their lives?

Pete left their small house expecting to return within a half hour. He arrived at the market just as two robbers were fleeing, having stolen forty-three dollars from the store owner at gunpoint. A police cruiser came screeching around the corner. Shots flew. Pete was hit in the neck and bled to death, right there in front of the store. He never got the cereal, and an eight-year-old Linda never got her father back.

She became a cop because of him. She named her business and her store after him. She idealized him, knew it, and had no regrets about it. She liked remembering her father from a child's perspective, with a child's adoration. It suited her just fine.

She left the police force after putting in her time and securing her pension. In quick order she opened her store, hired Mitchell Parsons to assist her (a godsend), moved to the woods of New Jersey, and hoped Kirsten would come along.

Kirsten, meanwhile, had watched Linda make her life changes and decided it was time to create new challenges for herself as well. She could see her fiftieth birthday rushing at her and was determined to make the coming decade her best. She'd founded and run McClellan and Powers Real Estate in New Hope for twenty-five years. Her business partner, Madeline Powers, was ten years her senior and had always wanted to buy her out—at least after their first decade building the agency into a local powerhouse. She proved eager to purchase Kirsten's half and remove her name from the awning, changing it overnight to Powers Real Estate LLC. There were no hard feelings between the women. They'd enjoyed an extraordinary run together and the trappings of success that came with it. But they'd never really meshed. They didn't have to; they were operating a business together, not a marriage. Madeline was delighted Kirsten had met someone new (even if she didn't think it would last). She liked Linda well enough, although the tall, direct-speaking detective was one of the few people she had ever met who intimidated her. She'd attended their very small wedding, and within a week she and Kirsten finalized the sale of the business. Then, to Linda's great surprise and relief, Kirsten she wanted to live in the woods, too.

Next came the issue of what to do in the woods. Linda had her store. Kirsten had a lot of money and no particular interests. Real estate was out. The sales had brought her many adrenaline rushes, but she was through with that. She tried working part time for Linda, but wasn't really into waiting on people. Besides, Mitchell was outstanding at his job, as she would expect from a fussy, single man in his forties who considered retail his life's purpose. She'd floundered for awhile, and had started wondering if a rural life was really best for her, when she came upon several old spiral notebooks in her boxes of belongings. She hadn't opened this particular box in years, keeping it in one of her closets, and she'd forgotten what was in the notebooks. She was alone at the house, organizing the garage where she'd put many of her things while she figured out what would fit in the house and what should be given away, possibly to *For Pete's Sake*. She took two of the notebooks out and went into the kitchen with them, settling in with a cup of coffee to take a look.

Stories. Poems. Attempts at journal entries that lasted a few days (she was never successful at journaling, but tried a few times because she had read that's what serious people do). It hit her then: these were her attempts at writing. Fiction writing. Storytelling. Word-craft. She had wanted to be a writer thirty years ago! It was a desire and a fantasy she'd completely buried in her storehouse of misplaced memories. They were beyond reach, but not far. And now, one Tuesday afternoon while rain fell outside the kitchen window on Lockatong Road, Kirsten McClellan knew what she wanted to do.

She'd been unsure how to proceed. Where does someone who hasn't written in years turn to when the muse suddenly shows up at the door asking to speak to the person at home? And what sort of writing should she do now, three decades after her last attempt?

Within an afternoon she'd read through those few spiral notebooks, cringing at the bad poetry, but impressed with two short stories. One was a romance ending badly and written about the same time her own heart had been broken by a girl named Cecile. She'd long since forgotten Cecile, and reading the story now made her smile. Love as foolish as it had been young. She decided to tell Linda about the notebooks, about her desire to see what creative spark was left in her, and if it could still light a fire.

Two weeks later she and Linda were having breakfast at the Star Diner in New Hope. As they were leaving, Kirsten noticed a flyer in the entryway on a small wooden stand by the door. Local merchants and people with services to offer left their business cards and flyers there. Kirsten almost walked past it, then stopped suddenly.

"Wait," she'd said. "It's a writers' group."

Linda let the door closed and stepped back in, reading the brief flyer along with Kirsten:

Have a story to tell? Waited long enough? The time is always write! New writers' group forming in New Hope, all are welcome. Give Melanie a call or an email and let's get started. Size is limited to twelve. Writing samples appreciated.

A telephone and email were listed. Kirsten took a piece of paper from her purse and fumbled around for a pen.

"Here," Linda said, handing her a ballpoint from her jacket pocket. She still carried a small notebook and pen, a habit she'd had all those years on the police force that still came in handy.

Kirsten called Melanie, whose last name was Johansen, the following morning. She wasn't too late, and she joined the fledgling group as its ninth original member. That was eight months ago. She'd since written three short stories and nearly completed the first draft of a novel. A Rox Harmony mystery, whose protagonist (never to be called Roxanne) appeared to be a mirror image of Linda Sikorsky, even to the point of being a registered Republican and having a father who'd died under suspicious circumstances when Rox was only ten.

Linda got used to Kirsten being gone on Tuesday evenings when she went to her writers' group. She also got used to Kirsten running plotlines and character ideas by her, even though Kirsten usually ignored her input.

"'Death Ahoy'?" Linda said when Kirsten told her the working title of the first book. "It sounds kind of ..."

"Cartoonish?" Kirsten replied. Her tone indicated that a "yes" response would have them sleeping in separate rooms for the night.

"Pulp-ish," Linda said carefully "Is that a word? 'Pulp-y.'"

"It's a working title," Kirsten sniffed. "It's not meant to be final. I know it has an element of caricature. I just needed a title, a handle for now. Of *course* I'm not calling it 'Death Ahoy.'"

Of course you were, Linda thought, *until now.*

And that's how it went for the six months Kirsten had been writing *Death Ahoy*, the working-title-only story of Rox Harmony, Private Investigator, taking her first cruise with a ship of lesbians, at least one of whom was a hired assassin with three kills under her belt before they hit international waters. Rox was named Roxanne at birth but forbid anyone calling her that. She was out to stop the killing and find out who was behind the brutally efficient murders.

Kirsten was in the home stretch now, down to the last few chapters and an epilogue. She'd heard from the group, who had christened themselves the Tuesday Scribes, about a retreat of sorts in Maine. Upon researching Serenity House, Kirsten learned it was really a glorified bed and breakfast in the coastal town of Cape Haven, catering to authors who wanted peace, quiet and a dependable internet connection. Melanie herself had spent a month there the previous summer finishing her collection of first-person essays about growing up in Pennsylvania. She vouched for the place as somewhere a writer can focus, if they could keep from being seduced by the Maine landscape—or perhaps because of it.

By August Kirsten was telling Linda they had to go to Serenity House (a name Linda said sounded like a last stop for alcoholics). By September the reservations were made. And by Friday morning, October 23rd, the women were packed and ready to make the six hour drive from their home in New Jersey to the Maine shore, checking into the B & B for four days of draft writing for Kirsten and sightseeing for Linda.

A serious storm had been forecast. Linda was slightly worried about driving in rain and wind that could get bad, but she was more worried about the blow to Kirsten's fragile confidence if the trip was postponed. She convinced herself they would make it without any problems. They could get an early start and be there before the worst of the weather.

Then her mother called from Philadelphia. Someone had broken into her apartment while she slept. Her jewelry was gone. The jewelry she kept in her bedroom. The thief had been there, alone in the dark with her, probably watching her sleep. She could have been killed, or something just as bad ...

Linda did not postpone their trip to Maine. She got in her car and drove the hour to her mother's home in Philly, setting them a good half-day behind schedule. It was a setback that changed everything.

3

HOWLING RAIN

THE ROOM had no working telephone; instead, a mustard yellow phone that looked like it came from the set of a 1960s TV show sat mute and useless on a creaky nightstand that threatened to topple over if Cayley touched it. The surface of the stand, as well as of the dresser with the large crack running diagonally across its mirror, had bubbled from moisture over the years and could be peeled off with little effort.

Everything about room #6 at the Cliff's Edge looked, felt and smelled old. Cayley guessed she was sitting among the original furnishings of the motel and that even when the place had been new, the furniture came second-hand. Probably from some other motel that upgraded when JFK was handling the Cuban missile crisis, or from a Goodwill that couldn't unload the stuff at must-go prices.

She'd done some research on the Cliff's Edge. First, there was no cliff. The motel was located along an inland stretch of Highway 1 north of Belfast, in unincorporated territory (as she'd been told by the greasy desk clerk) approximately three miles outside Lonesome Pointe. She had no idea why Russell Drover would name it something demonstrably untrue. His explanations died with him, and his death was why she was sitting on this bed, in this motel room, upset at being unable to get cell reception, unhooked from the internet against her will and better judgment, and angry at her source for possibly getting cold feet. He had abandoned her to this very bed, and now, for reasons she could not yet articulate, she was also upset that no one knew she was here. She'd wanted this story to be a bona fide scoop. It had all the elements of an exposé, something that would last more than a news cycle or two. It could spread far beyond Lonesome Pointe, Wathingham, and the small world in which the All Pointe's readers lived and died. This was nightly news stuff, New York Times stuff. She was going to be famous.

Her next step was to meet with the source in person. She would finally find out his name, something he had refused to tell her in his calls from a phone with a blocked number. He never said more than a few sentences at a time, offering his information in small packets.

She could tell by their second call the man was terrified. He kept making her promise she would not tell anyone, *anyone at all*, that he had contacted her or why. Not yet. Not until they'd met and he had convinced her the things he had to say were true.

"The walls have ears," he'd said when he called a second time.

"I'm not talking to you through a wall, Mr. ..."

He'd been silent, and she had wondered if her joke about a wall had cost her the connection.

"You won't think it's so funny, Miss Drees, when I tell you the story. The entire story."

"Please call me Cayley."

"I'll call you Miss Drees, and I'll let you know when you can call me anything. It won't be until we meet, that is for certain."

She'd felt her pulse quicken. "I'm going to meet you?"

"It only seems right, but when the time is appropriate. After I've given you enough information to make you sure of what I'm saying. Then we'll meet and I will offer you the missing pieces. I'll also tell you who I am. Hell, I'll show you."

He'd chuckled then and she had wondered if he might be dangerous in some way, or mentally unstable. It was a risk she was willing to take.

She'd pondered what he was telling her, which wasn't much at the time, as she tapped her pencil on the desk, hoping no one would come up to her cubicle just then. She had already decided to keep this to herself, whatever *this* was. At least until she had enough for a first draft story or a truly great pitch, the kind her boss Lucille could not turn down without the risk of Cayley going rogue and putting the story out there herself. She had no exclusivity agreement with the All Pointes. On the other hand, she was loyal, and she wanted to make her rise both legitimate and respected. Going to Lucille with a story and publishing it through traditional channels was her best bet at leaping up the ladder to star reporter.

You're getting ahead of yourself, Cayley, she'd told herself then. *All you have for now is a possible crank trying to tell you a suicide was a murder and it has something to do with a crappy motel nobody with any dignity would stay in. All the more reason to keep a lid on it for now. You could look like a fool.*

She knew the Cliff's Edge was a low-rent motel from the reading she'd done after the man initially reached out to her. First she had gone back and found the obituary she'd posted for Russell Drover, a short, to-the-point death notice sent in by his daughter, Dolores Platt (also named as his survivor, along with an ex-wife living in South America). Then she'd tried to find out about the Cliff's Edge, scene of the suicide that allegedly wasn't and a way station for the lost and tired with nowhere else to spend the night. She read a story a retired reporter did on the place's history, which in her opinion amounted only to rumor and speculation. There was no website for the Cliff's Edge, no Yelp or TravelAdviser reviews. It was as if the motel did not exist, or existed so far below the radar that those who stayed there did not want anyone to know it, for whatever reasons.

Embarrassment, probably, she thought to herself, looking around the room. Even the key the desk lizard gave her was plain and faded: #6. That's all it had on it, one of those diamond-shaped pieces of forest green plastic with a key attached. The door itself was just as old and used, with a flimsiness that made Cayley wonder why they bothered putting a lock on it. A good shove would open it.

Why are you thinking about shitty doors and people breaking in, she wondered. *What is it about this place that makes you shiver? Or maybe it's just the storm.*

It would be dark in a few more hours. The rain had begun again before she left the diner and was now falling steadily. She could hear the wind howling outside as it picked up speed.

She looked at her cell phone again, saw one quivering bar and cursed her lack of proper planning. She would never go on a blind date without anyone knowing where she was; why in hell had she come *here* without anyone knowing?

Correction, Cayley, she told herself. *He knows.* He being her contact, her source. He'd given her enough information over the last few weeks to confirm that the people in his story were real. She'd checked them out as best she could and no longer doubted they were connected, all participants in keeping deadly secrets that had their origins right here, in this motel of last resort outside a town that might not want its dead disturbed. She couldn't worry about that. She had more pressing things on her mind at the moment, like what happened to the only person besides the desk clerk who knew she was here. And how could she find out what happened to him? Had someone got wind of his betrayal and stopped him before he met with her for that final reveal, that dark heart of his tale? Or had he simply run off, regretting he'd ever made that call to tell her Russell

Drover had been helped out of this world?

She was relieved the hotel room lights worked, since nothing else did except a television with reception so poor the only point of watching it was for the sound of company. She was feeling more isolated at the Cliff's Edge than she wanted to be, more isolated than she'd ever felt. She told herself to relax, there were other people staying there. It wasn't as if she was alone in a farmhouse somewhere, or cut off in a cabin in the woods. She was fifty feet from a highway, in one of nine rooms that appeared to be occupied. She would be fine. At worst she would head out in the morning, back to the diner, or possibly to Lonesome Pointe. They would have cell reception, or a landline if it came to that. Something sturdy on someone's desk. Something that would get her back to civilization with a call to her boss to say where she'd been, or a call to her mother to tell her she was stopping over for lunch. She felt the need to be around someone who knew her well. She had the strange longing to be protected.

You're being silly, she told herself as she got up and closed the drapes. The parking lot just beyond the window was mostly full.

It wasn't that she did not want to look out on the storm; it was that she did not want anyone looking in.

4

BAD TIMING

LINDA HAD urged her mother for years to get an alarm system in the small North Philly row house she'd lived in since moving there with her second husband and daughter, when Linda was only ten years old. Estelle Sikorsky mourned the untimely death of her husband in Cincinnati and had sworn she would never love again, let alone remarry, but life surprised her; she met Kevin Carson at the local Presbyterian church the Sikorskys attended, and a year later she was moving east with him into the very house Linda rushed off to the morning she was supposed to be leaving for Maine.

Kevin had died ten years earlier in a traffic accident coming home from Trenton, leaving Estelle a widow for the second time. After that loss she kept her promise to herself and had not dated a man in the decade since Kevin's funeral. Instead she lived quietly and alone in their house on Lehigh Avenue where Linda grew up a second time (the first being the years before Peter Sikorsky was shot outside that corner market). The neighborhood's best days were already behind it when they moved there, but Kevin could afford the property and he swore it was on the upswing; gentrification would come to North Philly, you just watch. It never really did, and the area remained dicey, as Estelle called it, but it was home.

Pete Sikorsky and Kevin Carson were gun men—Pete for his job, Kevin for protection, and both because they were comfortable with firearms. It was a comfort passed on to Linda and her mother. Estelle gave Linda her father's military service Colt when she joined the New Hope police force. Pete had served in Vietnam with no regrets and no bitterness, at least none he ever spoke of. And while Linda never used the pistol on duty, she cherished it and gave it place of pride in her nightstand, where it remained in her new house on Lockatong Road and occasionally traveled with her.

Estelle preferred a shotgun, and had she been awakened by the intruder whose actions changed the course of that morning, and had she been able to reach the gun under her bed before the thief could stop her, she would have blown a hole in him and peered through to the other side without remorse.

There had been no warning, no time, and no waking up for Estelle. Luckily, all the thief wanted was the jewelry she kept in a cheap wooden box on her dresser. He'd grabbed her purse for good measure, then fled back downstairs and out the kitchen window.

"Ma," Linda said, trying to not let her anger show, "I told you so many damn times. You can't leave the windows open ..."

"But it's so nice out now, Lindey," Estelle said, using the lifelong nickname she'd had for her daughter. "The October breeze makes it so cool and fresh in here."

"It makes you a sitting duck," Linda said.

"I'll keep them closed and locked," Estelle replied. She was sitting at the kitchen table, clasping her hands to keep them from shaking. She was seventy-three but strong, proud, and determined not to let a burglar shake her more than he had. She'd even considered not calling Linda, but her purse was gone, her shotgun was unused, and, damnit, she was just so disappointed with herself.

Estelle looked to be about half the size of her daughter, whom she affectionately called big-boned. At five-five, she was middling height and she remained thin, having never carried more than a few extra pounds. She wore her gray hair long and tied back with a tortoise shell clasp. Her eyes were green, like Linda's; both women were direct, saying what they thought, when they thought it.

"I can't stay," Linda said. "We're going on a trip."

"I didn't expect you to stay," Estelle said with a bit of irritation. She was not a child and did not need anyone looking after her. She'd just been frazzled by the experience, and now she wished she'd dealt with it herself.

"Where are you and Kirsten going?" she asked.

Linda was used to telling her mother things several times, as she had about the trip.

"Maine. There's a writers' retreat in Cape Haven. Kirsten wants to finish her book."

Estelle kept silent. She was very fond of her daughter-in-law, but skeptical that anyone could succeed at a writing career this late in life—not that she knew anything about it. She'd learned long ago that it was best to keep one's opinions to oneself in most cases. Even with Linda's sexuality she'd bided her time, asking no intrusive questions. She'd never suggested a man for Linda, which should have told her daughter the conversation they eventually had would be brief.

"It's going to rain, isn't it?" Estelle said. "I saw it on the news. The whole eastern seaboard."

"I can't ask Kirsten to cancel. It's too late now anyway, we're supposed to check in tonight and we'd lose the deposit. Starving writers pay dearly for their retreats, let me tell you."

"Kirsten's starving?" Estelle said, startled. "Do the two of you need a loan? Are you losing money on the store?"

"We're fine," Linda said, wishing she'd kept her mouth shut. Her mother worried about her in ways she should not. Linda had always been frugal. Her store was doing well, or at least staying in the black. And she had plenty of savings. She just didn't want to take this trip and she had not admitted that to anyone.

"Listen, Ma, the police will be here soon to take a report. I have to go back."

"I'll be fine, Lindey. I'm awake now, and the shotgun's always loaded."

"You sure you don't want a sidearm?"

Estelle smiled. *Sidearm* is what Pete had always called his gun. Other people might encourage her to get a *firearm*, or a *pistol*, or a *handgun*. Linda, like her beloved father, called it a sidearm.

"I like the feel of a 12-guage," Estelle said. "And don't you worry, I'll be fine. I don't keep my identification in my purse anyway. The fool got away with very little."

Linda gave her a stern look. "'The fool' could have killed you, Ma."

"Well I'm sitting here talking to you, aren't I? Shoulda, coulda, woulda."

"You *shoulda* had an alarm system by now, and if you don't have one when we get back I'll have it installed myself."

"I'll get one. Now please, go. They say the storm's coming and I don't want the two of you driving in it, at least no more than you have to."

Linda looked at the clock above the sink. Her trip to Philadelphia had thrown them off two hours already, and would cost another two by the time they pulled out of their driveway. A morning departure would now be mid-afternoon and Cape Haven was a good six hour drive, if the traffic gods smiled on them.

"Call me," Linda said, hugging her mother. "At least twice: once after the police leave, and once after you call the alarm company.

Promise me."

"I promise."

Estelle got up to embrace Linda and the two of them walked toward the front door.

"Tell Kirsten I can't wait to read her book," Estelle said. "You must be so proud."

Linda hesitated and Estelle could tell there was more to Linda's feelings about it than she would reveal. It wasn't the writing itself; she was thrilled Kirsten had found a passion that would help her adjust to their life in the woods. She was not so crazy about having a character based on herself. There was something too intimate about that, something too *exposed*. She would reserve comment until she actually read the first draft. If Rox Harmony was too obviously Linda Sikorsky, then one of them would have to change, and it would not be Linda.

They hugged again. Linda kissed her mother on the cheek and squeezed her hand.

"Call," Linda said a last time, then she headed out onto the front stoop and closed the screen door behind her. If she did not hear from her mother by the time she got home, she would make the call herself.

* * *

The women were four hours behind schedule when they crossed from New Hampshire into Maine. Traffic had been heavy at first, with many people racing the bad weather to the safety of their homes. *Why are we doing this again?* Linda asked herself. *Oh, right, marriage. I forgot. In sickness and in health, in sunshine and in hurricanes.*

It was dark as she drove along Highway 1, following the coast north and east. For some reason she'd thought you couldn't go further east than New Jersey, as if the next stop from the Jersey shore was London. She wasn't geographically illiterate; she just didn't think of places like Maine as being closer to Europe. She'd never been to either, so maybe this was a sign of adventures to come. She hoped so, considering how unhappy she was at the moment.

She did not like driving after sunset; her vision had always been a problem once the sun went down—she had difficulty judging distances, and oncoming lights looked like bright yellow orbs surrounded by cotton halos. It didn't help listening to Kirsten talk almost non-stop about the novel she intended to finish once they reached Cape Haven and checked into Serenity House.

"Ship security was the big stumbling block for me," Kirsten said. She was eating spicy peanuts she'd picked up at a gas station just across the Maine border.

Linda was suddenly pulled back from her thoughts. She quickly recalled the conversation they'd been having, which consisted mostly of Kirsten bouncing plot ideas off her.

"Maybe they don't dock," Linda said, referring to the central story for *Death Ahoy*: 30 lesbians set sail on a cruise to the Caribbean, with one killer and Rox Harmony on the manifest. It had originally been an all-lesbian cruise, but Kirsten wanted to expand the possibilities by having a large group of women mix in as part of a regular cruise crowd on a much bigger ship. She'd turned the occasion into a reunion of older women, much like herself and Linda, who had all belonged to a gay women's volleyball league at different times throughout the 1990s. The women decided to have one last hurrah and set sail for a week of overeating and drinking to excess. What only a few of them knew was that their big celebration would be a deadly one, as first one, then two, then three of them began dying under mysterious circumstances. Enter Rox Harmony, who'd been in the league just out of college. Now a private investigator living in Philadelphia, she'd been contacted by the wife of the first victim, a woman who'd been shot coming out of the medical office where she worked. It wasn't long before Rox began to connect some very deadly dots, and off they all went on a ship where some of them were doomed.

"I thought of that," Kirsten replied. "But what kind of ship just sails for five days?"

"A trans-Atlantic one?"

"That would be a completely different story!" protested Kirsten. "No, no. Besides, it's called 'Bermuda Shots.' They have to go to Bermuda."

"I thought it was called 'Death Ahoy.'"

"That was always a working title. It's 'Bermuda Shots' now, as in Bermuda shorts without the 'r.' I can see the book cover, with the 'r' crossed out by a big, bloody red 'X.'"

"Don't you have to finish it before you worry about the book cover?" asked Linda. She was leaning forward now, peering hard through the windshield. The rain had begun to come down in sheets and she could barely see past her own headlights.

"I'm capable of doing two things at once," Kirsten said, her tone petulant. It was a side of her Linda had come to know well, and while she accepted it, she also avoided it whenever possible. Kirsten, like many writers, sometimes took herself too seriously. "Where was I?"

"Worried about the security issue on the boat."

"'Ship', Linda. It's not a boat at 140,000 tons."

"Ship, then."

"Yes. The authorities on the ship. The police. It's been a worry all along how to pull this off without getting the police involved, unless they stay onboard the whole time."

"So maybe they can't dock in Bermuda," said Linda. "There's been an outbreak of something on land."

"Yes!" Kirsten said, sitting up in her seat. "That's perfect! But not on land. *On the ship.* You just gave me the big plot point I needed for the last quarter. There's an outbreak on the ship. They can't dock—this isn't food poisoning, this is something viral—and the onboard authorities are completely distracted with this. Jade, the killer, panics, because now she's stuck on the ship, too. She can't make her escape in Hamilton as planned. She has to find another way off the ship now. And Rox is closing in. This is genius."

Kirsten's imagination was firing, with characters and storylines coming to life in her mind, when suddenly she shouted, "Watch out!"

The car broke hard as Linda jammed her foot on the break and veered to the side, almost running off the road.

"What the hell was that?" Kirsten asked, her heart racing.

"Something in the road," Linda said, as she slowly got back into her lane and drove on.

"An animal? What kind of animal is out in this rain?"

"That's a good question," Linda replied. "A better one is, what kind of *human* is out in this rain? We're not going to make Cape Haven, Babe. Not tonight."

"But I paid a deposit. We can't turn back."

"We're not turning back," Linda said. "Just call them and tell them we'll pay for the night and be there in the morning"

"Well," Kirsten said, "that's awful."

"Not as awful as dying on the highway."

They'd passed a sign a few miles back for a town called Lonesome Pointe. Linda couldn't remember if it was five miles ahead or twenty. She planned on taking the next exit when she saw a motel in the distance, off the road but not too far, with a blinking sign she couldn't read.

"We're spending the night there," she said, pointing.

"Where?" asked Kirsten, peering out the window. All she could see was rain, darkness, and a red neon sign about thirty yards off the road.

They came to a side road that looked more like a long driveway, and not far from the turnoff was a sign: The Cliff's Edge. Linda slowed and turned, making her way up the muddy road.

"Are there cliffs around here?" Kirsten asked, surprised.

"None we could get to without driving an hour," Linda replied. "Unless I got really off course, but I didn't. I'm guessing the owners were just trying to fancy the place up. 'The Cliff's Edge' sounds nicer than 'Crappy Roadside Motel.'"

As they pulled into the lot, which Linda was surprised to see nearly full, Kirsten took out her cell phone and made the call, surprised and relieved to get a connection in the storm. She told whoever staffed the front desk at Serenity House to please hold the room, they would arrive in the morning.

5

LAST ROOM AT THE CLIFF'E EDGE

LENNY SAW the car pull in. It was 7:30 p.m. now, dark and drenched outside as far as the eye could see, which was not far given the driving rain that had brought traffic to a standstill. The storm did not have a name but it was strong enough to be called something besides a Nor'easter. It deserved more respect than that. While it wasn't an Irene or even a Sandy, it was a nasty one and it packed a punch. That's why the Cliff's Edge was almost full. Lenny had worked the front desk for the past six years and had only turned on the "No Vacancy" sign three or four times. This just wasn't a place people looked for or added to their travel websites' favorites list. It was exactly what he saw tonight: a place folks ended up because they had to. Just like the two women who came in as he watched from his stool—wet, unhappy and stamping their feet as if the water were snow they wanted off them.

"Evening," Lenny said. "You ladies get stuck in the storm? Everybody else did."

"Yes, we did," Linda said. She regretted not bringing their rain ponchos, or at least a couple trash bags to put over themselves. Her jacket was soaked just getting from the car into the lobby, if it could be called that. It looked more like the front room in a house that should have been torn down decades ago.

"Well, you ladies are lucky tonight, let me tell you. I got one room left."

Kirsten hung back. She was still stewing over not driving on to Cape Haven. She'd been relieved to get a cell phone signal in this weather, knowing it was hit and miss. It wasn't great but it was good enough for her to tell the desk clerk they had to stop two hours short of Serenity House and they'd be there first thing tomorrow. The clerk curtly told her she would have to charge them for the night. Kirsten said go ahead, then filed it away for her Yelp review. She had no problem being charged, but she didn't care for being spoken to as if she'd inconvenienced someone with nothing else to do.

Linda looked at the skinny man behind the counter. She hoped he would not call them "ladies" again. She disliked the term and found it patronizing. Coming from someone who looked like his other job was pumping gas at the only station for twenty miles made it seem smug and deliberate.

"We'll take it," Kirsten said, stepping up next to Linda. She'd sensed her wife's hesitation, as if they had any choice but to check into the Cliff's Edge and get the hell out at sunrise. She just wanted to get into a room, settle in and fire up her laptop for some revisions on *Bermuda Shots*.

The clerk reached under the counter and brought up a key attached to a diamond-shaped piece of plastic with the number 7 on it.

"Last room at the Cliff's Edge," he said. "Lucky, lucky."

Linda had the distinct feeling their luck had run out, being forced into a rundown motel in the middle of somewhere.

"What town is this?" Linda asked, unsure they were even in a town.

"If it had a name," Lenny said, "It'd be Unincorporated. Nearest town is Lonesome Pointe, about three miles from here. That be cash or charge?"

Linda was surprised: she'd never stayed in a motel that took cash.

She pulled her wallet from her purse, slipped out a corporate AmEx and handed it to him.

"I'm Linda Sikorsky," she said. "And this is Kirsten, my … "

"Friend," said Lenny, winking at her.

Linda cursed herself and hoped Kirsten hadn't noticed the exchange. She glanced to the side and saw her furiously trying to get an internet connection on her phone. Good, the conversation had been ignored. She hated it that she was still uncomfortable referring to Kirsten as her wife. It had taken her months to get used to *partner*, and *spouse* was just too … animal-husbandry. She had to get past this. What difference did it make that some creepy desk clerk might disapprove of lesbians?

"Something like that," Linda replied, knowing Lenny had pegged them as a couple.

"Is there WiFi in the room?" Kirsten asked, frustrated at being cut off from the virtual world. The phone call to Serenity House was the last connection she'd had.

Lenny spoke patiently and slowly, as if to an uncomprehending child. "No," he said. "We don't have no internet connection here. This ain't Portland. But we got TVs you can watch. Not sure what kind of picture you'll get in this rain …"

"So it's not cable?"

Lenny did not respond, believing he'd made his point well enough. If the Cliff's Edge did not have an internet connection, why in the world would they have cable for the few people who stayed here? Mostly they came from surrounding towns to have sex with their secretaries or someone else's husband. Nobody had time for HBO.

"No," Linda said, answering for him. "I don't imagine it is. Let's just get our stuff from the car and settle in. It's going to be a long night. Isn't that right …?"

"Lenny," he said, handing her the credit card receipt to sign. "

"Does Lenny have a last name?" Linda asked.

Lenny felt the hair on his arms rise. The woman was not smiling, and there was an intensity in her eyes he didn't like. That's how predators looked at their prey. He knew, he was one. He'd looked at countless teenage girls and a few of the boys that way, usually before he got them high on something and screwed them. And he'd looked at old man Drover that way just before he'd put a hole in his chest. The girl reporter, too. But she was still in the queue. He suddenly didn't like putting these women next to the room Cayley Drees was in, but he didn't have any choice. It was the last room, after all. He'd be extra careful when he slipped into #6 sometime after midnight.

"You can just call me Lenny," he said. He was glad he'd talked Russell out of making him wear a name tag. What did the old fool think he was, a bellboy?

"Lenny it is," said Linda, handing him the signed receipt and taking the key.

"You ladies have a good night. And if you need anything, come on down."

"I can't call you from the room?" Kirsten asked as they were about to head back to the car.

"Phone works sometimes, but there's no intercom or nothing," Lenny said.

"Of course not," Kirsten replied. "Why would there be?"

Linda pulled the door open and held it for Kirsten. Rain flew into the lobby in the moment it took them to leave. Walking back into it was like walking into a powerful showerhead aimed directly at their faces. They got the last room, and they'd taken the last parking space, which meant they had to grab their belongings—none of which Kirsten was willing to leave in the car at this fine establishment—and hurry down the long motel front to room #7. Hopefully nothing would be damaged by the rain.

Lenny watched the door close. It was a lie they didn't have internet access. They just didn't have it for anyone but him, in the back apartment where Russell Drover had lived and where Lenny enjoyed his new life alone. *Linda Sikorsky.* He hadn't asked for her driver's license so he didn't know where she lived, but he could get the state off her license plate. He planned to see if he could find out anything about her online. There was something chilling in the way her manner had changed while they were at the desk, as if she, too, had sensed something about *him.* Two snakes who'd come upon each other in the tall grass. He had the unsettling feeling one of them would be eating the other. He hoped not; he did not want to draw attention to himself or, by extension, his employer. He wanted to take care of the reporter, see the women off in the morning when they turned in the key, and wait for it all to blow over. There was a fat paycheck and an extended stay in Puerto Vallarta on the other side.

6

UNLUCKY NUMBER SEVEN

LINDA WASN'T that troubled by the room; she'd stayed in motels like this one a dozen times when she was a kid travelling with her mother and stepfather. Kevin Carson had moved the family to Philadelphia for a regional sales job pushing medical devices to local hospitals. Sometimes he would take his family on his rounds, other times just his stepdaughter, as he zigzagged the Northeast trying to convince hospital administrators they needed whatever piece of machinery he was selling. Linda had loved it. Their trips alone had helped her appreciate her mother's second husband. He worked hard, he did his best; that his best would never get them in hotels much better than the Cliff's Edge wasn't his fault. Linda believed people had limitations, that's just the way it was, and the ones who accepted it were often the ones who did well in life, or at least were the happiest. She thought of an adage she'd always remembered: *Expectations are disappointments waiting to happen.* She expected nothing better from a roadside motel, and she was not disappointed.

Kirsten, on the other hand, was unaccustomed to staying in places that catered to the transient. Nothing in the room had cost the owner much, if he'd paid for it at all. The bed, the nightstand, the *carpet*, all had an indoor-outdoor feel to it, as if they could leave the dresser next to their car in a rainstorm and it would be no worse for it in the morning. It wasn't that Kirsten was a snob. It was simply that she had earned and enjoyed better things in life. Even when they'd flown frequently to Phoenix to be with Kirsten's dying mother, Dot, they'd stayed in the best hotel in town. (Kirsten's mother had moved to a one-bedroom apartment after her husband died, wanting as little to maintain as possible, and it was not large or comfortable enough for the women to stay there.) They were different in that way, among others: Linda's trips with her stepfather gave her a fondness for the unadorned, the simple, while Kirsten's childhood without plenty had made her want security, prosperity, and to never spend a night on a mattress whose cleanliness was in doubt.

"Are you sure we can't make it to Cape Haven?" Kirsten asked.

She was sitting on the bed with her laptop out. As promised by the front desk clerk there was no internet connection and their cell phones had stopped getting reception.

"It's only for one night," Linda said. She'd slipped into her pajamas and had turned on the television. It had been many years since she'd seen rabbit ears. These clearly didn't do much—the TV screen was filled with a grainy, barely perceptible rerun of *Cheers*. The volume was nearly to zero, since the sound was as bad as the image and Linda didn't want to drive Kirsten completely over the edge.

"Yes, well, it's going to be a long night."

"You could work on the book," said Linda. "Where'd you leave off?"

Kirsten looked at her. It wasn't quite a glare, but it was a look that said she'd already told Linda where was she was in the book and Linda should try a little harder to remember these things.

"Jade just killed the second person from the dinner seating," she said.

Jade (Kirsten had not yet decided on a last name) was murdering women from their 8:00 p.m. dinner seating on the cruise. One of those dining companions was private detective Rox Harmony. She'd seen an empty seat at the table for eight and seized the opportunity to get very close to her target. Sometimes the universe worked to your favor, especially if you were a novelist in need of a plot twist.

Three of the women at the table that first night had a dark connected history only Jade was aware of and had committed to erasing. Harm had been done, debts incurred, and Jade was there to collect, if Rox couldn't stop her in time.

"Rox knows what Jade is up to," Kirsten said patiently. "Evelyn is now dead, but only Jade knows that for sure, and only Rox suspects. The ship's authorities are quietly investigating, since there's no body and no proof that Evelyn's done anything other than vanish, which isn't that hard on a ship with two thousand other people. Maybe she's in someone's state room. Maybe she jumped into the ocean, disappearing in the ship's wake. Rox is going to find out, and do what she has to to stop Jade from claiming another victim."

"I'm hooked," Linda said. Listening to Kirsten's plotting and character questions had been part of their conversations for the past four months.

"I knew that the first time you smiled at me," Kirsten said. She looked at Linda as the mood lightened. "Two years this New Year's

Eve."

"Has it been that long?" Linda said. They'd met at a mutual friend's party celebrating the turning of another year. Linda had only been out a few months. She'd always known she was a lesbian, but she had never done anything about it until recently, and she never imagined meeting someone so soon afterward. She discovered to her surprise that she was ready for love and the challenges that came with it. They'd met those challenges. They'd married, moved to a small country house a mile from the Delaware River, and here they were, waiting out a storm in a crappy motel somewhere in unincorporated territory several miles from the coast of Maine.

"You can turn the volume up," Kirsten said. She closed the laptop and set it on the floor. "I'm going to read a book."

Linda took the suggestion, raising the TV's volume some, but not much. She wasn't really interested in the grainy show with the bad sound, and she liked listening to the rain. It had slowed, but not enough for them to keep driving. She didn't want to leave now anyway. She wanted to settle into bed, next to the woman she knew she would spend her life with, and slowly drift off to sleep.

* * *

She didn't know exactly what woke her up. It happened sometimes: she would be lost in a dream she would not remember moments after awakening, but something about it would disturb her and send her rushing to consciousness. It was as if a dream had been too real and she'd needed to escape it, despite her inability to recall what the dream had been about or who had been in it. These were the emotional consequences of the mind attempting to talk to itself in symbols, to sort things out, to warn away. And now, in what could truly be called the middle of the night, she lay on her side, awake, staring into the darkness.

Kirsten did not wake up when Linda stirred despite the stillness of the room. The storm had died down to a slow drizzle. Up until they'd gone to sleep they could hear the wind howling and rain lashing everything in its path. But now ... 3:00 a.m. by the nightstand clock (the room's only amenity besides the useless television and a phone with no dial tone) ... all was quiet. She was awake and uncertain of returning to sleep. This happened sometimes, more frequently than she liked, although she never liked it. Most times she could drift back to sleep in a half hour or so, but other times not, and she would quietly slip out of the bedroom and start her day. But that was in their house, where she had other rooms to go to. Here she had only the bathroom, and she was not about to spend two or three hours in there.

That was when she heard the sounds. Muffled, from the room next to them: #6. It had to be #6 because that's how the rooms were numbered along the single-story motel, #1 through #9. The Cliff's Edge was not a large motel and was never meant to be. They'd taken the last available room, according to the desk clerk. She sat, trying to identify the sound coming through the wall. A thud, then something heavy being moved. A television being turned off. She knew it was a TV because she'd heard it when she'd turned off their own.

Then the sound of a door opening. She was curious, but she still did not want to get out of bed and risk disturbing Kirsten. The last thing she needed was both of them awake three hours before sunrise. She lay in bed and listened. She heard a car trunk close, but not slam, as if someone was trying to be quiet. At this hour people would probably keep the volume down so they didn't bother anyone trying to get a good night's sleep. Finally, the sound of a car motor turning over, followed moments later by wheels on gravel, the sound receding as the car slowly pulled away.

She shrugged it off. Whoever it was just wanted to get an early start. She couldn't blame them: she and Kirsten would never have stopped here had they not been forced to, and she intended to hit the road as soon as they had breakfast.

She slowly turned on her side, closing her eyes and hoping sleep would come again. Another hour would do. She knew the dream of Diedrich Keller would not be back tonight—it never occurred more than once in a night, as if teasing her. Here then gone, laughing in the darkness as it fled from the arrival of consciousness.

Time to let go, relax, prepare in the morning, and get the hell out of here. The sooner she saw the Cliff's Edge in her rearview mirror, the better.

7

IN THE LIGHT OF DAY

MORNING BROUGHT sunlight and clear skies. Storms are often like that—big, threatening and ominous when they arrive, replaced by cloudless expanse when they're gone, leaving only debris as evidence they'd been here. This one was no exception. Had they named it? Did it need to be a certain magnitude before meteorologists and TV reporters in the scare trade called it Doris or Joshua or Umberto? As far as Linda knew, it had just been a *Nor'easter,* the generic name for large storms battering the Eastern seaboard. They'd been ill-advised to drive to Maine in those conditions, but Kirsten's heart had been set on getting to Cape Haven and finishing her novel. And it wasn't as if this was a hurricane or a blizzard, just a large, nasty storm that had forced them to find shelter early, two hours before they would have reached Serenity House. Here, in this almost-roadside motel that looked even more decrepit in the morning sun.

"I'm starving," Kirsten said.

She was by the bed packing the small suitcase she'd brought for the trip. Linda was at the window, looking out between the drapes she'd pulled apart. She hadn't opened them completely, not wanting to flood the room with light. It was especially bright this morning, as if reminding everyone that storms come and go but the sun always remains.

"There's a diner a couple miles back," Linda said. "Marge's, I think the sign said."

"*Back?*" said Kirsten. "Do we really want to go back instead of, you know, on to Cape Haven?"

"It's two miles, maybe three. We'll have a good breakfast, come back and check out, then get on our way. We'll be at Serenity House by noon. And just because I love you, we'll stay an extra day if we can keep the room. Make up for the lost night."

"Thanks," Kirsten said, "That's very sweet of you. I already called them when you were in the shower and booked an extra night. But I appreciate it, almost as much as I appreciate getting cell service again."

Linda wasn't bothered. She had adapted in very short order to being half a couple. It wasn't something she'd ever imagined for herself, except for the occasional day dream or flight of fancy. But she liked it, she liked it *a lot*. Linda Sikorsky, married to Kirsten McClellan. If not two of a kind, then two for one. One love, one life, one road trip to Maine.

Still looking out the window, Linda noticed an empty space in the parking lot. It wasn't next to their car—they had parked close to the front desk, trying not to get soaked in the twenty seconds it took them to get inside.

"There was a car there last night," Linda said, her head cocked as she stared at the empty parking spot.

"What?" asked Kirsten. Linda had spoken softly, talking to her herself.

"A car. There was a car in the spot in front of room six. A Camry, I think, kind of gold-ish."

"Kind of 'gold-ish'? It's gold or it isn't."

"Gold, then," said Linda. She knew there was no logical reason to stare at the spot, except she remembered the sounds she'd heard in the middle of the night. This must have been the car that left. Why would anyone leave at that hour? Was it any of her business? And why did she care? Something just felt off about it, something she would never know because they were leaving. They had a trip to make. Kirsten had the first Rox Harmony Mystery to finish.

Linda stepped back from the window. "I'm starving, too," she said. "Let's go eat. Leave everything here. We have to come back this way anyway, we'll settle up then."

"There's nothing to settle up," Kirsten said. "He charged your card last night. I'd just as soon never see him again. I felt like a fly being eyed by a spider."

"Me, too. But I have to give the key back. It's not a plastic key card they can just keep printing out."

"There's a slot in the door, I saw it. You can drop it in there."

"While he watches me from the front desk? No thanks. Let's just go and deal with it after breakfast."

A moment later they stepped from the room into the morning sun. The sky was almost painfully blue. The air was crisp, October-cold, and smelled amazingly clean.

They walked fours cars down to theirs. Linda opened the door for Kirsten, a gesture Kirsten always found romantic, even though

Linda opened the door for pretty much anyone getting into her passenger seat. It still sent a small thrill through Kirsten.

They pulled out of the parking lot, down the road onto Highway 1 and drove back the way they'd come, both of them eager to see the sign for Marge's Diner.

* * *

Marge's Diner was exactly what you'd expect for a roadside eatery. America was dotted with them along its highways and off-ramps. Some were large, with 10-page menus sending the diner into a frenzy of indecision; others, like Marge's, were small, not much bigger than a railroad car, with a half-dozen vehicles parked outside.

Linda and Kirsten were sitting in a booth having just been served coffee by a waitress from Central Casting. Her name tag said Betsy and she looked like she'd worked there since the grand opening thirty years ago.

"I still don't know about the climax," Kirsten said, stirring slightly curdled creamer into her coffee.

"What don't you know?" asked Linda.

"She has to confront Jade, obviously. Protagonist has climactic encounter with antagonist. But does she *kill* her? Would you, having been in that situation before?"

Linda looked at her. She'd accepted that Rox Harmony was based on her, but she bristled when Kirsten came too close to her own lived experiences.

"Without hesitation," she said, her tone indicating an end to this line of inquiry.

"Sorry, Babe, I'm just trying to figure out my ending. I mean, I *know* the ending. It's one of the rules of writing I've learned from the group, and it helps tremendously. I know where I'm going, I'm just not quite sure how to get there."

Betsy returned with their breakfast, both women getting eggs, toast and bacon. Betsy put the plates down. She took a moment and arched her back, placing her hand behind her and pressing as if in pain.

"Long morning?" Linda asked.

"Long night," said Betsy. "I pulled a double, maybe a triple, I lost track of time somewhere around lunch yesterday."

"It's a hard job," Kirsten said.

Betsy was about to walk away when Linda suddenly asked, "So you were here all night?"

"Twenty-four hour diner," Betsy said. "Somebody has to be."

"Let me ask you something," said Linda. "Did anyone come in early this morning, like, *early* early? Around, say, three a.m.?"

Betsy thought about it, then shook her head. "Nobody. We only get some truckers that time of the night. Had maybe two guys in here. Why?"

"No reason, I was just curious. Somebody in the room next to us left in the middle of the night and I thought maybe they stopped in here to fuel up, get some coffee to go."

"No, just the two truckers." Betsy turned away from them. Then, remembering something, she said, "I saw that young reporter's car drive by. Thought it was an odd time to be going anywhere, but she didn't stop."

"So how come you noticed?" asked Linda.

"Because she was so nervous when she was here for dinner last night. Anxious. And you can see the road from here. Just about no traffic at that hour, especially right after a storm. I noticed it, that's all."

"Was she from around here?"

Linda could tell she was annoying Kirsten with all the questions, but she couldn't let it go. The whole night had bothered her; something wasn't right and this was the only way she could address it.

"No," Betsy said. "She was from the All Pointes Bulletin, up in Wathingham. Local rag. Everybody gets it, nobody reads it."

"Sounds like the New York Times," Kirsten said.

"She say what she was here for?" Linda asked.

"No," said Betsy. "We didn't have that much of a conversation. Just chatter, you know, like I have with the customers. The ones I need to get back to, if you don't mind."

"Well, Betsy," said Linda, "thank you for the information. You notice what kind of car she drove?"

"A Camry, I think. Gold."

Gold-ish, thought Linda. The car she'd seen parked outside room #6. The car that left in the middle of the night.

"You ladies need anything else?" Betsy asked.

"No, thank you," said Linda. "We're fine."

Betsy nodded and headed back to the counter. She was the only server on duty and she'd just lost valuable time talking to the two women from out of town. She knew all the locals, and these two weren't among them.

Kirsten dug into her food while Linda moved hers around on the plate. If she was hungry, it was for information, not eggs and toast.

"I'm glad we're leaving," Kirsten said. "We can make Cape Haven before lunch, and we can check in. The room was ours last night, so there won't be any wait."

Linda spoke without looking at her, not wanting to see Kirsten's reaction.

"Just a slight wait," she said. She couldn't see Kirsten's disappointment but she knew it was there.

"For what?" Kirsten asked.

"I just want to talk to that desk clerk again."

"The lizard."

"That's the one."

"What do you want to talk to him about?"

"The car that was there last night and isn't this morning."

"Let me guess. The gold Camry Betsy saw drive by."

"That would be the one."

"I don't like this," Kirsten said, sliding her plate away. She'd eaten one egg and a piece of bacon."

"I just want to ask him some questions."

She had not told Kirsten about the dream of Diedrich Keller. She had not told her about waking up at 3:00 a.m., or the sound she heard in the room next door, or the car driving away. She hoped this did not count as deceit. She and Kirsten were honest with each other and had been from their first date.

"Fine," Kirsten said, her tone indicating it was not. "You ask the creep a few questions, we turn in the key and we hit the road. I have a novel to finish."

And I might have a puzzle to solve, Linda thought, adding it to the things she did not tell Kirsten.

8

BACK SO SOON

LENNY WAS exhausted. He hadn't slept, and he'd walked two miles back from where his boss dropped him off after helping him stage the death. Meredith Vesey didn't take chances, and she would not be seen with Lenny anywhere near the Cliff's Edge or a recognizable approach. She had not participated in the murder—that had been Lenny's job, and he'd accomplished it with remarkable ease. Cayley Drees had been asleep when he entered her room, and barely awake when she realized she was being strangled. By then it was too late. She did not call out (an impossible task with an extension cord around her neck). She had struggled only briefly before pissing herself and going limp, the kind of limp that said she was dead. He'd wanted to fuck her but decided it was too great a risk, and too time consuming. Besides, corpses weren't responsive and he preferred a struggle. Even someone as impulse driven as Lenny Winfrow had the sense to be quick when it mattered. Luckily she was a small woman, and once he'd wrapped her in a dark plastic garbage bag it had been no great task to get her to her car, where he'd placed her in the trunk. From there he drove out to Old Hickman Road, where Meredith was waiting.

"You're late," she'd said.

Her Mercedes was parked a half mile away—she did not want any other tire tracks to be found.

"Not by much," he'd said.

He'd driven the last hundred yards without headlights and thought himself lucky not to run over the old dyke. He was sure she was one, too, although Meredith had never officially announced any such thing. She didn't need to. The town folk filled in the blanks: woman in her 50s, never married, dressed like a man. C'mon, of course she's a lesbian. He didn't mind. It wasn't his place to judge, and he'd had a few especially fun sexual experiences with bisexual women, usually in threesomes. He had more respect for people who just came out and said what they were instead of leaving it up to rumor. Meredith Vesey was not one of them. But she was rich and powerful. To Lenny's mind that's all that mattered.

"She put up a fight?" Meredith asked, peering into the car under the mistaken assumption the girl would be in the back seat.

"She's in the trunk," Lenny said. "No fight at all. You said be quick about it and I was. How'd you know she was coming to the Cliff's Edge?"

"What I know and how I know it is my business."

Lenny assumed she had an informant, one of many she paid just like she paid him. That's how Meredith operated. It didn't help that the Drees woman had made inquiries she thought were discreet but that set off alarms to people with secrets to keep, like exactly how Russell Drover met his end.

He could see the contempt in Meredith's eyes. He knew what she thought of him. He knew what everyone thought of him, even the kids he romped with once they got whatever meth or crank or pills he had to offer. Fuck 'em. That was his motto, and he usually did.

"Let's get this over with," Meredith said, looking at a watch Lenny figured cost an easy grand.

He proceeded to carefully take Cayley Drees out of the trunk, unwrap her and place her body in the driver's seat. This was going to look like an unfortunate accident, that was the plan.

"Ah, Jesus, Winfrow," Meredith said, taking at look at the body. "She's got marks on her neck!"

"Course she does," Lenny replied. "That's what an extension cord will do to you, you pull it tight enough."

"This is a problem."

"Not a problem at all, Boss. The car goes into the ditch, slippery road, danger everywhere, and what do you know—it catches fire! Fire destroys evidence."

He could see by her expression she was not convinced. She'd begun pacing back and forth along the car's length.

"Change of plans," she said. "No fire. Cars don't just explode! You've watched too many goddamn TV shows. No, this can't go that way."

He was losing his patience by then. It was cold and still very wet, and he wanted to get home.

"What you got in mind?" he asked.

After thinking quietly another moment, during which she remained absolutely still, Meredith said, "Rape. Strangulation. She gets left twenty yards or so from the road. You'll have to take her pants off."

He'd dressed the body before taking it out of the room. Clothes were essential if they were faking a car accident.

"Then what?" he asked, hoping she'd say he had to rape her to make it authentic. He had a condom in his wallet in the event of such an opportunity.

"We leave the car here as planned. They'll figure she stopped to help someone who got stuck, or maybe she picked up a hitchhiker. Or somebody forced her off the road, that happens. They'll find the car, then the body, and it'll hit the news for maybe a couple days. It'll be a cautionary tale for young women everywhere: this is what can happen when you go driving on a dark road at night. It's not that uncommon."

She stood back, having no intention of touching the dead woman, and told him to hurry.

"Don't you want me to …" Lenny said.

"To what?"

"You know, make it real. Fuck her."

"She's dead, for godsake!" Meredith said, horrified the little ferret would even suggest such a thing.

He saw it then—the fear in Meredith Vesey's eyes. She hadn't fully realized who she was dealing with when she hired him. Now she did. He saw her reflexively reach for her purse where she kept a 9mm Luger in case of emergency. He'd seen it before, and he knew she'd shoot him if she felt too threatened. He suddenly wondered if that was her new plan: come upon a sexual assault while she was out driving for some reason. She sees the woman's car, stops to investigate, finds Lenny on top of Cayley Drees and, BANG!, shoots him dead.

"What are you waiting for?" Meredith asked. "The sun will be up in another hour."

He shrugged off his fantasy and got to work.

Fifteen minutes later Cayley Drees was laid out in a field, naked from the waist down. The car was wiped clean. The very first rays of light could be seen as a shadow slowly filling the far horizon, and Lenny was in the passenger seat of a Mercedes, heading quickly back to a spot two miles from the Cliff's Edge where Meredith would drop him off and he would walk quickly home.

He saw the women pull up in front of the motel. He figured they must have gone out for breakfast, probably at Marge's since there wasn't anywhere else to go. He watched them get out of the car and head to the entrance. He liked the big one, but he didn't trust her. Something dangerous about that one. He would be glad to see their taillights heading out and away.

"Morning," he said as Linda and Kirsten came through the door. "You ladies headed out today? Good day for it. It's always nice after a storm like that, you ever notice?"

Kirsten stood back, and Lenny could tell he made her uncomfortable. He'd noticed it when they checked in.

"You're good to go," he said. "Just need the key."

Linda walked up to the desk, deliberately close to him. She'd deduced the night before that he could be intimidated, if it was done carefully.

She casually placed her palms on the desk, leaned even closer, and said, "I was wondering about the room next to us."

"What about it?" he said, his smile instantly gone. "You're talking about room eight, is it?"

"No," said Linda. "The other side. Room six."

"Well," Lenny said, "I can't tell you much since that's an unoccupied room."

"Hmm. I was sure there was someone in there when we checked in."

"That's impossible, Ma'am. Room's been vacant for a week now. Last couple stayed in there, they ... how can I put this? They made a mess. Got a little too hard into the partying and trashed the place. I'm still getting it fixed back up."

Linda knew he was lying. And she knew, in that moment, something was very wrong here. Something *Detective* Linda recognized immediately as having criminal potential.

"I woke up early this morning, very early, and I distinctly heard sounds coming from that room."

"I don't mean no disrespect," Lenny said, "but I'd guess you was dreaming. Only sound you could have heard from room six was maybe a rat digging through all the trash those people left in there."

"That you haven't cleaned up for a week," Kirsten said.

"I been busy."

"I bet you have," Linda said. She turned to Kirsten and added, "You know, I like this place, and we didn't get to see much of the area."

"You're not serious," Kirsten said.

"Oh, Sweetheart," Linda said, knowing it would intrigue the lascivious desk clerk and possibly throw him off guard. "We'll get to Cape Haven in plenty of time. I'd just like to spend the day, see Lonesome Pointe." She turned to Lenny. "How come they call it Lonesome Pointe?"

"They don't call it that," Lenny said. "That's the name of the town. As to why, it's got one lighthouse. Somebody long ago must've thought it looked lonesome. And there you go."

"There we go indeed. I'd love to visit that lighthouse, and whatever else they've got in town."

She could see the alarm on Kirsten's face. She was pushing her luck and would have to finesse the situation later as best she could. She would try to get them on the road by evening, but she wanted one day to find out the truth of what was going on at the Cliff's Edge.

"I'll have to charge you, you want to stay the day," Lenny said.

"Oh, that's perfectly fine," said Linda. "We're on an expense account. My wife here is a writer, a novelist, in fact. We're exploring the area. Any suggestions?" She was pleased with herself for calling Kirsten her wife this time.

Lenny had slid his stool back, wanting more space between them. "No suggestions," he said. "Nothing to see. Small town, couple stores, a lighthouse. You'll be finished by lunch."

"Let's hope so," Kirsten said. She then turned and left the office, letting the door slam behind her.

"Yes," Linda said, smiling at Lenny. "Let's hope so."

She kept the room key she'd been planning to turn in. Feeling Lenny's stare on her back, she headed out and followed Kirsten to the room.

9

TROUBLE IN PARADISE

"WHAT THE hell was that about?" Kirsten said.

They were back in their room. The small suitcase Kirsten had packed was standing upright in the corner, its handle extended, waiting to be wheeled out to the car. Her laptop was snug in its case on the bed. The only thing left to do was leave; now they were staying and Kirsten could barely contain her frustration.

"It's just for the day," Linda said.

She was glad she'd left her phone plugged into the wall. There were only two people she carried it for—three if you counted her store assistant Mitchell—and she'd already spoken to her mother when Kirsten was showering. (The house alarm had at last been installed and Estelle wanted to be sure Linda memorized the code. She planned on resetting it when they got back: 1234 was not much of a secret PIN.) That left Kirsten who was standing just inside the doorway with her hands on her hips, looking down to contain her upset.

Linda watched her take several deep breaths, her eyes on the floor. It was a way of calming down and it usually worked.

Finally Kirsten said, "So what do you want to do now that we're staying here?" She'd relaxed and was no longer hiding her expression. She knew Linda could read her thoughts on her face and she had not wanted to start this trip—a trip they'd already delayed—with an argument.

"I want to take a little trip," Linda replied.

"To Lonesome Pointe? You really want to see a lighthouse and a general store, or whatever they hell they have there? Maine's full of lighthouses, Linda."

"I think we'll skip the lighthouse."

"So what are we doing then?"

Linda held up the thin newspaper she'd picked up at the front desk. Small towns everywhere seemed to have their own versions: local news, announcements of fairs and exhibits at the town library, if there was one, and lots of advertisements.

"I'd like to visit the All Pointes Bulletin."

"The *place?*" Kirsten said, not understanding.

"No, Babe, the *newspaper.*"

She held the paper up and poked it with her finger.

"Why don't you call them instead?"

"For one thing, I doubt they're open yet." It was only 8:30 a.m. "For another thing, I like an element of surprise."

"Where is this newspaper located?"

"In Wathingham," said Linda. "Our waitress Betsy told us that at the diner. And it's just about a hour, maybe ninety minutes from here. I checked."

Kirsten frowned. "I don't like this, Linda. I don't like it at all."

Linda took a breath. "Listen, you're writing a mystery. You hope it'll be a series. You have a character—based on me, for godsake."

"Your point is?"

"Watch and learn, my precious scribe. Listen and learn. I haven't been crazy about Rox Harmony being a thinner, younger Linda Sikorsky, and that's okay. But if you want to do this, then come along. I'll show you how this detective stuff works."

Linda knew Kirsten couldn't argue with that and was even excited by the prospect. Kirsten had never asked her about her work as a cop, not in any probing way. Linda didn't like to talk about her job. Kirsten had asked some questions as she developed her central character: what's an interrogation like, do they leave bodies in place while they work a crime scene, can they really process DNA between commercial breaks, but she had never gone for a ride-along, so to speak. This was a chance to be with Linda, by her side, while she worked what may be a case or may prove to be a waste of their day. The possibilities were intriguing.

"What's at the All Pointes Bulletin you're looking for?" asked Kirsten

"Not a *what,*" said Linda. "A *who.*"

"A *who* who drives a gold-ish Camry, I'm guessing." Kirsten looked at her watch. "Let's get going then, I want to be in Cape Haven by sundown, if not sooner. I have a cruise ship with several dead bodies waiting to be discovered."

"To Wathingham we go," Linda said.

She took her phone and pulled the charger out of the wall.

"Let's take everything. That way you'll know we won't be staying again, and reptile man won't have anything to steal."

Linda could see the tempest had passed. She took the suitcase by the handle while Kirsten scooped up her laptop and they headed to the car.

10

THE VIEW FROM HERE

THE VESEY house could be seen from any location in Lonesome Pointe, provided you looked in its direction. Originally built by Theodore Vesey in 1926, it commanded the top of a hill facing the ocean just two miles away. You could stand in the roof garden (now an expanse of cracked tiling and debris from three generations of a dying family) and see the shore with its single unused lighthouse that gave the town its name.

The Vesey family had been among the community's founders, back in the late 1800s. Maine is small in population and was even smaller then. Most people yearning for expansion and opportunity headed west for territories still unknown, wild and filled with possibilities, failure high among them. Maine was for people who'd already been there since its beginning or had ties to the land. Once part of Massachusetts, Maine gained statehood in 1820, entering the Union as a free state as part of the Missouri Compromise. And while often thought of as little by people who don't know any better, it's the largest of the New England states, bounded by New Hampshire to the west (making it the only state to be bordered by just one other) and Canada's Quebec and New Brunswick provinces to the north. It's also the eastern-most point in the United States.

Meredith Vesey knew all these things but gave them no thought. Why would she? She was not in the tourism business and never had reason to promote a state known by most for ex-presidents, lighthouses and lobsters. Her family history was barely more significant to her. Theodore Vesey was her great-great-grandfather and existed only in a painting above an unused fireplace in a large dining room she never used. The last remaining Vesey, Meredith kept the house for its value and the lingering sense of power it gave her in a town that never grew. Everyone in Lonesome Pointe knew who Meredith Vesey was, much of it spoken in gossip: She was a lesbian who'd never come out, they said; she lived alone in that big, creaky, windswept house for reasons that must be suspect. Why would any normal person live there? What were the secrets she guarded so closely?

She'd just got off the phone with one of those secrets and she was not pleased. She told herself she should have known better than to hire the fool for work this important. She should have brought in someone from Portland, or maybe Boston. She would have had trouble finding men who do what she'd needed done, but they were out there. She'd taken an easy way, and now she regretted it.

"Could be nothing, could be something," Lenny had said on the phone. "They said they were just gonna tour the town, see the lighthouse, but I don't know, Boss, something about the big one bothers me. She's nosy."

"How so?" Meredith had asked, staring out the living room window smoking a cigarette. It was one of the nice things about living alone—you could smoke in any room and not be hounded for it.

"She asked about room six, who stayed in it."

"And the significance of this is what, Lenny?"

She'd wondered if he was masturbating while they talked. She wouldn't be surprised.

"That's where the reporter was!" he said, as if she were dense. "The one ..."

"I know the one," Meredith snapped. "We left her in a field."

She'd started pacing, crushing out one cigarette and lighting another. "Maybe she was just curious."

"Like a snake's curious about a mouse," he said. While mentally dull, his instincts were sharper than most.

"Do you have a name for this curious woman?" Meredith asked, wanting to get whatever information she could from him and hang up. She disliked speaking to Lenny Winfrow almost as much as she disliked being around him.

"Yes, Ma'am, I do. Got it written down. Her name is Linda Sikorsky."

"You know where she's from?"

"New Hope, Pennsylvania," he said. "Used a corporate card for some store there when she paid for the room, looked it up this morning. It's a safe guess that's where they're from."

Linda had used her store's credit card to charge the room, knowing she could do some shopping for saleable items and write off the trip.

"Good job on that, Lenny," Meredith said as she stopped

pacing. She'd always known praise was an effective treat, like biscuits for a dog. "Was it just the two of them?"

"Oh yeah," he said. "It was her and her ... now get this, Boss ... she called the other one her 'wife.' That crazy or what?"

She had the feeling she was being baited, and she didn't like it.

"Same-sex marriage is legal now, Lenny," she said. "What you think of it doesn't matter."

She knew he thought she was gay. She knew the whole town thought that. She didn't care and she had never been one to meet the expectations of her inferiors. They were sheep and she was the wolf, let them chatter among their sheep selves. As for Lenny trying to push her buttons, she knew how to push back if she needed to.

"Listen, I have to go," she'd said, wanting to be off the phone with this creature. "Don't do anything for now. Just wait for my instructions."

"Yes, Ma'am."

"And stop calling me 'Ma'am.' I hate it."

"Yes ... Boss."

'Boss' was better, but she didn't like that, either. Being known as Lenny's boss could get her life without parole. She'd hung up the phone then and gone to her computer, where she began searching for a Linda Sikorsky in New Hope, Pennsylvania. There was a website for a 'vintage everything' store, some place called *For Pete's Sake*. To Meredith 'vintage everything' just meant a second-hand crap shop. She didn't patronize them and would never be in this one, but it provided her one crucial thing: an About page.

She began reading about Linda Sikorsky. She learned the store was named after Sikorsky's father. She learned the wife's name was Kirsten McClellan. And she learned that Linda Sikorsky had spent just over twenty years with the New Hope Police Department. Lenny had been right to worry, and now Meredith Vesey was worried, too.

11

THE ALL POINTES BULLETIN

TOO BIG to be a town and too small to be a city, Wathingham, Maine, sits equidistant between Lonesome Pointe and Cape Haven, almost precisely ninety minutes from each. Linda knew this from watching the map on her dashboard GPS system. She'd been following it since they'd left the Cliff's Edge and hoped Kirsten hadn't paid much attention to the glowing roadmap. She was wrong about that and knew it—she could tell from Kirsten's deepening silence that she, too, had watched their progress as they headed north toward Cape Haven. She worried Kirsten would start pressuring her to drive on and be done with it.

Wathingham had grown over the century and a half of its existence. Originally a small inland settlement, it became in the 1950s the home of Wathingham Tasties, "America's Cracker," with a factory that employed five hundred people at the height of production. You could once find Tasties on nearly every table in the country's diners, ubiquitous salted wafers people enjoyed in their soups, salads and with any number of dips and spreads. They were also a favorite of women who thought stuffing their purses with crackers was expected of them, and certainly not criminal. (Old man Sid Wathingham, the last owner of the factory before it went extinct like so many other American manufacturers, once said the company had been kept afloat thanks to sweet grandmothers and respectable wives stealing his product.)

Now emptied of many of its young people, Wathingham managed to hang on by sheer determination. Its population had held steady at twelve thousand. A new generation of 20- and 30-somethings who called whatever they did "artisanal" had discovered the pleasures of rural Maine and were escaping with their families from the big cities of Portland and Boston, helping keep the town alive. The two main streets now boasted free-trade coffee shops, organic bakeries, and at least one vegan grocery store, mixed in with the ancient mom-and-pop stores, a Salvation Army thrift store, and a row of antique shops.

"This place is kinda cute," Kirsten said as they turned onto Hester Street, Wathingham's central artery.

"I think the whole state is like this," Linda replied. "They might even have two lighthouses here."

"We're too far from the shore," said Kirsten. "There's no reason to have a lighthouse where there aren't any ships."

Kirsten was right. She was also suddenly interested in their surroundings, which relieved Linda of some of her worry and guilt about coming here.

"Where is this place?" Kirsten said, meaning the All Pointes Bulletin's office.

Just then, the robotic but benign voice of the GPS tracker spoke up. Linda called the digital woman Maggie.

"*Your destination is ahead on the right.*"

"I think we're here," said Linda. She saw a two story office building with no signage on it and pulled into a parking space, of which there were plenty. Apparently, the little newspaper that served the surrounding towns was not a major tourist stop.

"Get me the roll of quarters, Sweetie," Linda said, turning the ignition off. Her car, a beige Mitsubishi Galant, circa 2000, was old enough to still use a key. She'd ridden in newer ones that were keyless and did not look forward to buying one when the Galant finally sputtered to its death. There was something about a car without a key that felt too space age to her.

A minute later they had inserted enough quarters for an hour and headed inside the building.

There was no guard. A sign on the wall listed several businesses, including a dentist, a hair removal salon, and the All Pointes Bulletin on the second floor. They took the elevator up, encountering no one else, and stepped into a large office that was so quiet Linda wondered if they were closed.

"Hello?" Linda called out.

The reception desk was empty but its computer was on. Linda heard crying from down the hall and considered walking to its source, but she did not want to alarm anyone.

"Can I help you?" a young man said. He looked distraught as he hurried to the front desk. He was wearing khakis and a blue shirt and tie. Linda guessed he was the receptionist when he went behind the desk and addressed them from there.

"Is this the All Pointes Bulletin?" Linda asked.

A sign on the wall behind the young man said it was, but she still thought it best to ask.

"Yes, it is. I'm Rudy. Can I help you with something?"

A loud wailing erupted from somewhere down the hall.

"Is this a bad time?" asked Linda.

"You haven't heard?" Rudy said.

The women did not listen to news when they drove. Mostly they played music, and sometimes audiobooks, but seldom news unless they were looking for a traffic report.

"Heard what?" said Kirsten. Her curiosity was evident and Linda guessed she had forgotten all about Cape Haven for the moment.

"Cayley was found dead this morning." Rudy spoke as if they should know immediately who Cayley was.

"I'm so sorry," Linda said, deliberately giving the impression she knew who he was talking about. "We were just coming to speak to her. This is terrible."

She did not feel unethical in the least. Her years investigating deaths, many of them homicides, had taught her that much could be learned from feigned familiarity. Something told her the young woman who had dined at Marge's the night before, driving the car waitress Betsy had seen go by in the middle of the night, was the one named Cayley.

They heard crying again, and voices.

"Is the manager here?" Linda asked.

"The editor, you mean?" Rudy said.

"Yes. He—"

"*She*. Our editor is a she. Lucille Proctor. Who did you say you were?"

Linda knew she had to be careful. If she appeared to be obfuscating or outright lying, walls could come up. She did not have time to work her way around them.

"I'm a writer," Kirsten said, stepping up to the desk. "My name's Kirsten McClellan and I'd been in contact with Cayley about a book I'm writing."

This seemed to pique his interest. Maybe he, too, was an aspiring novelist. Or maybe he was just an accommodating young man.

"I'll tell Lucille you're here," he said. "I doubt she'll have much to say, under the circumstances. Please, have a seat."

There was a small knee-high glass table about six feet from the desk, with three beige fabric chairs that looked like they'd been purchased at Ikea twenty years ago. Linda and Kirsten walked over and sat down, waiting while Rudy headed back into a maze of cubicles. Linda could see him turn into an office. She had to think quickly. She didn't know Cayley's last name, and she would soon be pretending they had come to see the deceased woman.

"Thanks, by the way," she said to Kirsten. "That was very quick thinking, about being a writer."

"I am," replied Kirsten.

"Of course you are. I meant it saved the day, or the moment at least. I was about to do my retired-detective routine on him, and there's never any telling where that will lead."

"Considering she's been murdered, it could have complicated things."

"Who said she was murdered?"

"I know you very well, Linda. If you didn't think she was murdered before we got here, you do now. And you know something? I do, too."

A moment later they were approached by a woman who looked to be in her sixties, and all business. Her button-down sweater was thick with pockets the size of oven mitts. She wore a tan blouse and a skirt just one shade darker that brushed her knees. There was a diamond wedding ring on her finger, but Linda knew instantly this was not a *Mrs.* Anyone. Proctor was probably her maiden name and the one she would always use.

A first glance at her and Linda knew Lucille was a tough old bird, the sort who belonged in a place as rugged as Maine and who, without doubt, did not abide fools or falsity long. They would need to play this as well and as truthfully as possible. It was time for Detective Linda to make an appearance.

12

LUCILLE PROCTOR

LUCILLE PROCTOR stood nearly as tall as Linda, close to six feet in stockings that were nestled into low-heeled shoes. She was not the one who'd been crying loudly in the back: her face was set, well-lined and unmoved by emotion. Rudy did not attempt to introduce them, instead motioning to the women seated in the front area, then heading to the back to continue grieving and consoling.

Linda and Kirsten both stood when Lucille walked up to them.

"May I help you?" Lucille asked.

"My name is Linda Sikorsky," Linda said, extending her hand for a quick shake. "This is Kirsten McClellan."

"Lucille Proctor. I'm the editor of the All Pointes, as well as the publisher. Rudy said you were here to see Cayley Drees."

Linda was relieved to know the dead woman's last name.

"Yes," Kirsten said, inserting herself in the conversation. "I'm writing a novel set in Maine, and Cayley was going to give me some information."

Lucille stared at Kirsten. Linda could tell they were being quickly sized up.

"What kind of information?"

"About the area, about Maine."

"Where did you say you were from?"

They hadn't said, and Linda knew they needed to be honest.

"We're from New Jersey. Pennsylvania, originally, but now New Jersey. I was on the police force in New Hope for twenty years, a homicide detective the last six."

Lucille's eyes widened slightly. "Homicide. What a coincidence. The thing is, Detective ..."

"Retired."

"Retired, then. The thing is, I don't believe in coincidence. So why don't you tell me why you're really here?"

A moment of truth had arrived. They could continue to fabricate a story about coming to talk to a reporter for information they could have gotten from anyone living in the area, or they could lay their cards out, face up.

"I think Cayley Drees was in the room next to ours at the Cliff's Edge," Linda said.

Lucille cocked her head a moment, curious. "That old motel outside of Lonesome Pointe?"

"That's the one," Kirsten said. "We stayed there by accident."

"Interesting. How does someone stay anywhere by accident?"

"What Kirsten means," said Linda, "is that we got waylaid by the storm. We're actually headed to Cape Haven. We got a late start yesterday and the worst of it hit us on the road. We had to stop for the night."

"And you think Cayley stopped for the night, too. It's only ninety minutes away. Why would she spend the night there?"

"I'm hoping you can help us figure that out," Linda said. Then, carefully, she asked, "How did she die? Did it say on the news?"

Lucille Proctor took a moment and Linda saw for the first time how deeply the death had affected her. Even steel can be bent, she thought.

"They haven't said yet. But I'm going to assume it was foul play. She was found in a field not far from her car. That usually means the worst. Please, come into my office and we can talk while you show me your identification."

"She's retired," Kirsten said.

Lucille turned to lead them back to her office, and said, "I'm not doubting that. I just want to know you are who you say you are. This is a newspaper, if you hadn't known before you got here."

Tough as hell, Linda thought, feeling a deep respect for the woman they were following down the hallway.

* * *

The walls in Lucille's office were bare. There were no paintings, no prints, no photographs of the editor standing next to any mayors or prominent citizens. There were also no windows: it was an interior office surrounded by cubicles, copy machines, two ancient faxes, and a small pantry the staff used for taking breaks and drinking coffee. The All Pointes Bulletin's seven full time employees all wore several hats: reporter, ad salesperson, promotion department, and online content provider. Only Rudy had one job, as receptionist and office gofer.

"It's not the New York Times," Lucille said. She continued observing Linda and Kirsten as they sat at a small round table in her office. "Everyone here does everything. That included Cayley Drees."

"What I'm wondering," Linda said, "is if one of the things she was doing led to her death."

Linda expected this to surprise Lucille but it didn't seem to. *Intrigue* would be a better word. The editor looked as if the thought of her young reporter being killed on the job was a remote possibility. Horrific, tragic and most unusual.

Kirsten remained silent. She was the one who'd lied, saying she'd been in contact with Cayley when she had not known the young woman existed until they walked in the door. She knew enough to let Linda take it from here; she wanted to see how it was really done, how a detective, retired or otherwise, worked. She did not expect *Bermuda Shots* to be the last of the Rox Harmony mysteries. She'd already made a short list of ideas for books two and three. The more she could study the professional moves of her wife, the more realistic she could make her central character.

"Why do you think her death is connected to her job here?" asked Lucille.

"I can't really say," replied Linda. She did not want to call it instinct, but that's what it was. "I think, but I can't prove yet, that she spent the night in the room next to us. She was at a diner called Marge's, just a couple miles down the road, and a waitress there saw her car drive by very early this morning, well before sunrise. I'm just wondering now if you could tell us what she was working on."

Lucille thought for a moment, then said, "Obituaries."

"Obituaries?" said Kirsten, breaking her silence.

"Well, that and selling ads and covering local mom and pop events. She was relatively new here—she'd interned last summer and for some reason I can't fathom she wanted to work here. She was so bright, so talented ..." Lucille choked up, ever so slightly. "There's nothing about her job here that would get her killed."

"Nothing at all?" Linda asked.

"The dead don't kill anybody, Ms. Sikorsky."

Oh, but sometimes they get *you killed*, thought Linda. "Why obituaries?"

"It's an entry level beat, that's why. And it doesn't take much in the way of writing. People submit obituaries for their loved ones. All we do is an occasional polish, grammar and spelling, that sort of thing."

Linda could see Lucille thinking, trying to recall something.

"There was ...," said Lucille, "something. I don't know exactly, but Cayley had become secretive the last few weeks."

"How so?" asked Linda.

"Not sneaky, exactly, but as if she was hiding something. She would click her computer screen off if I walked up. Other times she would shut a folder she was looking at and slide it under the papers on her desk."

"You never looked at it when she wasn't there?" Kirsten said.

"I'm not a snoop," said Lucille. "I'm an editor. I've done plenty of reporting in my time, but I don't invade my staff's privacy."

"What about phone calls?" Linda asked.

"Yes, actually, that too. Several times she got calls and went into the pantry. She'd close the door and talk in there. I assumed she was seeing someone and didn't want anyone to know yet."

"Man or woman?" Linda asked. As a former detective, she did not bother with niceties or worry about people's prejudices. Facts had no biases.

To Linda's mild surprise, Lucille said, "She wasn't family, if that's what you mean."

Linda had not been in the gay world long, and really wasn't now. She and Kirsten didn't go to bars, didn't hang out where so many other gay men and lesbians did, but she knew instantly what "family" meant; she knew, too, that Lucille Proctor was one of them. It was not a comment that needed pursuing. Instead she said, "Would the young man at the front desk know about her phone calls?"

"Only if they came through the main line. But we can ask ...."

Lucille got up from the table, leaned out of her office and called out, "Rudy! Rudy, could you please come in here?"

Rudy shuffled quickly down the hallway and into the office. Lucille closed the door behind him. This was not a conversation she wanted whispered about in the office.

There was not a fourth chair at the table, so Lucille stood and motioned for Rudy to sit.

Linda thought he looked like a child called to the principal's office. A child who'd been crying five minutes earlier.

"Rudy," Lucille said. "This is Detective Linda Sikorsky and her friend. You met them, obviously, but Ms. Sikorsky has some questions for you. And everything said in this office stays here, yes?"

"Of course!" Rudy said.

Two thoughts immediately came to Linda: one, that Rudy was the sort of hyper-efficient young man who took his job very seriously and two, that she did not have any questions prepared.

Rudy turned to Linda, his hands gripped in his lap.

"Yes, well," Linda said, thinking as quickly as she could. "What I'm interested in are any phones calls, any contacts, Cayley Drees may have had the last few weeks."

"Phone calls?" he said. "She gets lots of phone calls. Her mother calls every day. I don't imagine she'll continue doing that."

He looked as if he was about to cry again.

"Focus," said Lucille. "It won't be more than a few minutes, we promise."

"Mostly your regular calls, that's all," Rudy said. "She had her cell phone, she used that as far as I could tell. People might call here for her, then she'd give them her cell phone number to use. It was on her business cards under the main number."

This concerned Linda. If the answer to Cayley's death was on her cell phone they would not get far. That would be left to the authorities investigating the case.

Rudy thought a moment, then said, "There was this one guy … He called two or three times through the front desk. I thought it was odd."

"How so?" said Linda.

"Well, for one thing, the number was blocked. Not many people still have blocked numbers. And he was just … I don't know … strange. I'd put him through to Cayley, who he called 'Ms. Drees,' even after asking to speak to her a couple times."

"The first time, too? Did he call her that the first time?"

"No, as a matter of fact," Rudy said. "The first time he called he asked for, and I quote, 'whoever writes the obituaries.' We don't write them, *they* write them—the people who send them in. If they need us to, we have a template for it. So I transferred him to Cayley, and that's how it started."

"How what started?" asked Lucille.

"I don't know, exactly. Just that Cayley got very hush-hush

about it. Like she was doing something she didn't want anyone to know about. You think she was selling drugs?"

"Of course not!" Lucille said. "And don't you dare put that into anyone's head around here. She wasn't selling drugs. When reporters get tight-lipped, it means one thing: she was working a story."

"What makes you think that?" asked Kirsten.

"I'm an editor, and if I'm any good, I know when one of my reporters is working on something."

But you didn't know when she hid the file and shut her computer screen off, thought Linda, knowing she could not say it.

"What obituary was he calling about?" Linda said, wanting Rudy to focus again.

"I don't know," he replied. "We run them from the surrounding towns and counties. Maybe three or four a week. I read them."

Lucille: "You read them?"

"As, you know, a hobby."

"No, I didn't know. But don't be embarrassed. A good obituary is an art form. We don't get many of those, but it's not an unusual pastime."

"Were any of them connected to the Cliff's Edge motel outside Lonesome Pointe?" Linda asked.

He looked at her, remembering the obituaries he'd read. "Yes, actually. One of them was."

Eureka, thought Linda. "Who died?"

"The owner, some old guy, I don't remember his name … wait, it was Drover."

"Russell Drover," Lucille added. "Crusty old son of a bitch, he came in here a few years back complaining we ran a profile of the property. He said it was unflattering, cost him customers, which was ridiculous since the only customers he got were the lost and the lustful."

"What was unflattering about the story?" Kirsten asked.

"I didn't write it," Lucille said. "It was Jeb Harris. He's retired now. But there's a history to the property, at least as far as I can recall from the piece. The Cliff's Edge wasn't high on my list of things to care about."

"It was a farmhouse," Rudy said.

They turned to him: he'd either read the story or knew the information from local lore.

"Way before my time," Rudy continued. "Back in, like, the forties or something. Then it was sold to some woman who put up the motel. People in the community hated it. They said it attracted the wrong kind, whatever that means."

"What else did the story say?" Linda asked.

"I don't remember, exactly. There's a whole history to the place. You'd have to read it yourself. I could get it from the online archive and print it out for you."

"Please do. But before you go, what about the obituary?"

"Pardon?"

"Russell Drover's obituary. What did it say?"

"The usual. He was survived by a daughter, loved by pretty much nobody. It didn't say that, but I'm good at reading between the lines."

"It's your hobby," Lucille said.

Ruby blushed.

"Was there more?" Linda asked.

"Not really. There wasn't anything about a viewing or a wake, or even a funeral. It's what it *didn't* say that was interesting."

"And what was that?"

"That he'd killed himself," Rudy said, as if they should know this. "The obituary said he died. That's all, just died, with a date. But word travels around here."

"He's right," Lucille said. "Suicide makes juicy gossip. And I remember now. Old Russell Drover shot himself in the back office of that place. I think he lived there, I'm not sure. But depending on who was telling the story, he either shot himself, hung himself, or had himself dismembered."

"Who would know, exactly?" asked Linda.

"Well, Russell himself," said Lucille, "but he's not talking. The other people would be the medical examiner, the mortician, and Jon McBride. He's the sheriff in Lonesome Pointe."

"They have a sheriff?" Kirsten asked.

"You women really aren't from around here, are you?" said Lucille. "Yes, we have sheriffs, for the county. Some places even have police departments, depending on the size of the town." To Rudy she said, "You can go now, and thank you. Just remember …"

"Confidential."

"Absolutely."

Rudy left the room. Lucille did not close the door this time.

Linda got up from the table, signaling Kirsten to do the same. "You've been very helpful, and you didn't have to be. It's much appreciated."

"Oh, I expect something in return," Lucille said, smiling. "I'm an editor, you'll recall. I have a paper here that's been struggling, oh, about thirty years now. I want to know who did this to Cayley as much as anyone, but I also know it's a story, Detective."

"And you want to tell it."

"Yes, as a matter of fact I do. I want justice for Cayley, and I want the bastard who did this to be written about, in detail. Every single thing about him, there for all to see. That's what I want."

"Exclusively."

"Always."

She stepped aside to let them out of her office. "By the way," she said as they were about to leave. "Sheriff Jon McBride is family. His husband's a deputy there, there's no secret about it. He's a nice man. But discreet, if you know what I mean."

Linda knew exactly what she meant. She'd been discreet herself for many years, what others call closeted. She still did not want to see it that way, and she fully understood the implications: small town sheriff, gay, but quiet about it. Maybe it would help her when she spoke to him, maybe it would not.

Lucille walked them to the front door. Rudy was back behind his desk. He handed Linda a print out of the story they'd run on the Cliff's Edge, as well as a copy of Russell Drover's obituary.

"Interesting stuff," he said.

"Interesting enough to get someone killed," Linda replied.

Lucille saw Rudy's startled look. She pressed her fingers to her lips and said, "Remember, confidential."

"Absolutely."

Linda and Kirsten thanked her a last time and left the All Pointes Bulletin office. It was now almost noon and Linda knew she'd made a promise to be in Cape Haven by nightfall.

13

A TRUSTED SOURCE

MEREDITH KNEW people in high places, few of them friends and most of them wary of crossing her. Lucille Proctor was certainly among the highly placed and not someone Meredith had ever considered approaching or extorting, but her receptionist, Rudy? He had an unfortunate willingness to betray his employer.

Rudy had called her less then five minutes after Linda and Kirsten left the All Pointes office.

"I gave them a copy of the story Jeb did on the Cliff's Edge," he said.

Meredith remembered it. It was what started this whole sorry affair. Digging into a past no one wanted to see again never came to any good. *Closure*, perhaps, for those who believed in it, satisfaction for some, but more often it brought unintended consequences. When she'd read Jeb's story, with its history of the property, the quick exchange of ownership and all the gossip and speculation that surrounded it then, she knew her disdain of reporters was well founded. Jeb Harris escaped by retiring—what point was there in silencing a man who had already spoken? She wished people who found snake pits fascinating would just stay away from them. Jeb had come to peer over the edge and backed away, but that young reporter had stepped right into it, a fatal move.

"I'm grateful for the call, Rudy," Meredith had said. "Your mother's mortgage payment will be good for another six months—assuming that's what you use the money for."

"Oh, absolutely, Meredith ..."

"Miss Vesey, please. I'm your employer, not your friend."

"Miss Vesey," Rudy said, correcting himself. "The money has been so helpful, I can't tell you."

"Then don't, Rudy. Just keep the information coming when you have it. There's a cash envelope waiting for you in your glove compartment."

That was how she'd paid him the past two years. On designated days he would leave his car on a side street, well away from the All

Pointes office and its windows offering views of the parking lot. Meredith would have one of her trusted underlings make a very quick deposit in his glove compartment using the spare key Rudy gave her when they first agreed to do business. Poor Rudy, with his mother on disability all these years. She'd been within a month of selling the house Rudy grew up in, the house where his father's wake was held, the house where his mother endured two miscarriages before being blessed with the miracle of a son. Meredith knew the value of information—perhaps the most important weapon in anyone's arsenal. She knew Rudy's situation, his mother's dire straits, and she offered to help. Quid pro quo, with the quid being $500 a month as a retainer. Thanks to Rudy, very little went on in Webley County that Meredith did not know about.

"I think you should know," Rudy had said before Meredith could end the conversation, "they were headed to Lonesome Pointe."

"I would imagine so, Rudy. The Cliff's Edge is there, or near it."

"That's what I'm trying to tell you. They aren't going back to the motel."

Meredith felt a lurch in her stomach.

"I can do without the suspense, Rudy. Where are they going?"

"To the sheriff's office. I heard it through the intercom. I'm afraid she's going to catch me someday."

"That's what the hazard pay is for. I can always look for someone else."

"No, no, please, I'll take the risk."

The lurch Meredith felt at the news became a free fall. Who was this woman, this Linda Sikorsky? Why would she care what happened in a town as small as Lonesome Pointe? And what could Meredith possibly do to stop her?

She knew Sheriff Jon McBride. Her attempts to carefully initiate a similar arrangement with him, should she ever need to be in his good graces, had been quickly cut short. McBride did not take bribes disguised as donations to a favorite charity, and he would not hesitate to pursue criminal charges against anyone who did. The Sikorsky bitch meeting with McBride could be harmless, since he knew much of the speculation about the Cliff's Edge and nothing of the truth, or it could be the beginning of something bad.

"What's Lucille think about any of this?" Meredith had asked.

"Nothing, as far as I know," Rudy said. "We're kind of busy

with this awful Cayley Drees situation. It's horrible, Miss Vesey. Have you seen it on the news?"

"I have, Rudy, and I am so, so sorry for you all. I'm sure she was a very nice person, and a good young reporter."

"The best," he said, and his voice caught.

"Go now," Meredith said, ending the call. "Grieve, I know you need to. And don't worry about more information for the moment, you have a tragedy to deal with. I'll take it from here."

"Thank you, thank you," Rudy said. "Take care."

"Oh, I will," Meredith said, hoping her words had not sounded cold.

It was time to call the rodent again. But first she had to decide on a plan of action. Lenny Winfrow was lethally good, but equally stupid. She could not set him to another task without knowing exactly what the results would be.

"Dolores!" she called out.

"Yes, my love," Dolores said from the living room.

Meredith knew she'd been listening and she didn't care. They were as far into this together as they could be, and she wanted no plausible deniability from Dolores Drover. If things headed south she would not go there alone.

"It's time for a new plan," Meredith said.

Dolores came into the sun room where Meredith had taken the call from Rudy. Three years her junior, Dolores looked a good ten years older than Meredith. Frumpy, with lips ringed by smoker's lines, thirty pounds overweight, long brown hair that always looked as if it needed washing, Dolores would be considered a catch only by the desperate or the vision impaired. Luckily for her, Meredith had been desperate six months ago—desperate, angry and determined. All it had taken to change things was a sweetheart card from the drug store and a dozen roses sent to Dolores's home in Bangor. Everything made right with a postage stamp, a florist and a lie.

Dolores kissed her on the cheek. "I'm all ears," she said, taking a cushioned seat next to Meredith in front of the bay window. "Should I get a pen and paper?"

"No, that's fine, Darling," Meredith said. "Remember, nothing ever gets written down."

They sat in silence for several minutes, enjoying the sun on their faces. Finally, Meredith began to tell her what they were going to do.

14

LONESOME POINTE

LONESOME POINTE was neither lonesome nor a pointe. Founded in 1836 by a fishing family named Leeland, the community had been known successively as Seasight, Pinder's Landing, and even Leelandville before the Leelands left for Massachusetts over a grudge in which they had taken one side and everyone else in town had taken the other. They packed up their name and left soon after, settling somewhere near Rockport where they were quickly absorbed and forgotten. The only thing remaining of the clan was the myth that its matriarch, Jessica Leeland, described the town's single lighthouse as lonesome. "Oh, look at that poor lighthouse," she was believed to have said in the mists of legend, "It looks so lonesome." Whether Jessica Leeland had ever said this, and whether she had even existed, did not matter. The townspeople liked their oral history and this bit of it had stuck, as had the name the community eventually took for itself.

Linda and Kirsten arrived at the entrance to town approximately forty-five minutes after leaving the All Pointes Bulletin. Linda was known to break the speed limit, a risky maneuver in a place where small municipalities relied on speeding out-of-towners to help meet their budgets. Fortunately for Linda, and tragically for Cayley Drees, the morning's murder had preoccupied whatever law enforcement there was in the area. At least that's what Linda told herself as she slowed down, looking at the surprisingly wide central thoroughfare in front of her. She noticed it was not called Main Street.

"Kind of reminds me of New Hope," Kirsten said. She'd been quiet most of the ride, except for telling Linda several times to slow down.

Linda did not agree but refrained from saying so. New Hope was larger than Lonesome Pointe and significantly more artsy. There were also no motorcycles here clogging the roadways, roaring through the hills like wasps. Bikers loved the Pennsylvania and New Jersey countryside. It seemed they weren't much attracted to Maine.

"It's cute, that's for sure," Linda said.

And it was: River Street, an incongruous name for a street where there was no river, winded like an elongated 'S' through the heart of town. Driving between its two ends the women could see an ice cream shop, several dress shops, a diner, two small-town restaurants, and a Starbucks in competition with a Kool Beans on opposite corners.

"What do you think the population is?" asked Linda.

"One thousand, two hundred and sixteen, as of the latest census," Kirsten replied. She'd gotten the information on her iPhone while they were driving.

Lonesome Pointe, while not the county seat, housed the county sheriff and its six deputies. Kirsten had read this online as well, preparing herself for whatever Linda had in mind to do here.

Webley County, no doubt named after another founding family, was the smallest in the state, with Wathingham being its biggest and only city. Maybe, Linda thought, this was the Sheriff's Department's way of being polite to the Wathingham police—out of sight, out of mind—or maybe, like so much of life in Maine, it had simply been tradition to operate here. Whatever the reasons, Linda knew the large, two story building just beyond the town's 'S' was where the Sheriff's Department was located. She drove to it, paying no attention to the stores they'd passed. There was no time for exploring, with a possible exception for a coffee stop when they left.

There were two Sheriff's patrol cars in the side lot and a half dozen civilian cars. Flags of Maine and the United States flew at full mast in front.

"It's big for a small town police department," Kirsten said as they pulled into a slot and parked.

"It's a sheriff's office," Linda explained. "It serves the county, not just Lonesome Pointe, which doesn't seem much bigger than the parking lot. But it looks like New Hope!"

"No, it doesn't. I wasn't looking closely. It looks about half the size, if that. And I don't get the feeling many tourists come here, except the drive-through kind."

They both stretched when they got out of the car. They'd spent much of their morning in it and were looking at several more hours of driving before they could end their day in Cape Haven.

"What are you going to say to them?" Kirsten asked. "Any ruse to get you past the receptionist?"

"It may be a deputy," Linda replied. Many police stations had officers at their front desks. She had no idea if it worked that way here, or if they would encounter a civilian—he or she—staffing the front entrance. Whoever was there would be armed, openly or discreetly, she was sure of that. Not everyone who came to a sheriff's office was there to drop off a bag of fresh muffins to say "Thank you" for their service to the community.

Linda made a quick appraisal of the building: two stories, flat, yellow-beige. It looked big enough to accommodate ten or more rooms on each floor. She knew from her time with the force at least one of those rooms would be for records. Another would be a large kitchen where deputies could decompress, eat, talk, and, in days long gone, smoke. The sheriff himself would have a large office—open seating arrangements had been trending in police stations long before they made it to the corporate world, but a sheriff's conversations could be delicate and privacy was still important. And there would surely be a holding cell of some size. This was not the county jail (Linda didn't know if they had one in Webley County and wasn't about to send Kirsten on another iPhone search to find out), but there would be space for at least a few detainees. People drove drunk, they acted out in public, they assaulted other people, and the Sheriff's Department had to have a place to temporarily store them.

The sun was directly above them in a sky completely different from yesterday's storm and darkness. Linda wished they'd left a day later, or that they weren't taking the trip at all, but they did and now they were walking into the sheriff's station. There was no turning back. She wanted to know for certain that Cayley Drees was the woman in room 6 and what exactly happened to her between the time Linda heard a disturbance at 3:00 a.m. and the time an unfortunate driver found her car with her body twenty feet away.

The lobby of the sheriff's office was large and modern. It felt more to Linda like the lobby of a medium-sized corporation, or the front office of a law firm without dark wood paneling. There were hallways leading off to each side of the front desk, but little else. She could sense activity, but she had no feel for how many people worked here or how busy they were.

Kirsten hung behind as she'd been doing all morning. Linda wondered how much of the day's actions would end up attributed to Rox Harmony in Kirsten's second novel.

An older woman sat at an island front desk: there was no wall behind her. She looked to be in her fifties, and Linda pegged her as the sort who had been here since graduating college, or possibly high school. A name plate on her desk announced her as Gayle Sellers. She was dressed like a woman her age, in a light blue blouse and a tan button-down sweater that was not buttoned, revealing a small gold Star of David around her neck. She smiled at them as they walked up to the desk. Linda recognized it as the smile of a woman who knows her position and the quiet authority that comes with having held it for thirty years. Linda guessed she was armed, probably with an efficient and lethal handgun in her desk drawer.

"May I help you?" Gayle asked, quickly and expertly appraising the two women who had just approached her desk.

"I was hoping to speak with Sheriff McBride," Linda said.

"Do you have an appointment?"

"No, unfortunately. I was referred to him by Lucille Proctor at the All Pointes Bulletin, about that tragic murder this morning, the young reporter they found."

Gayle's eyes narrowed slightly. "Who said it was a murder?"

"I was just ... well ... you're right, it might not be. But given the circumstances, it doesn't seem likely she was thrown from her car."

Gayle said nothing for a long moment. Linda worried she had somehow offended the woman, or stated her reason for being here too bluntly.

Finally, having waited long enough to make both Linda and Kirsten squirm, Gayle said, "Well, it would help if you told me who you are."

"Yes, yes, of course," said Linda. "I'm so sorry. My name is Linda Sikorsky, and this is my friend, Kirsten McClellan."

Linda knew she would hear later about calling Kirsten her "friend" but she wasn't going to worry about it now. Kirsten may wish to live in a world where one woman introducing another as her wife did not raise eyebrows or stoke prejudices, but Linda knew better. People were free to make assumptions, and all of them did, but she would not invite resistance when she needed answers and cooperation.

"That's a good start," Gayle said. "But it's not much to go on, or to tell me why you should see Sheriff McBride without an appointment."

Linda made a judgment call. This was not some young receptionist who would tweet out the first juicy piece of gossip she was offered, or hurry to a water cooler to tell her office companions.

"I'm a retired homicide detective," Linda said. She quickly took her wallet from her purse and pulled out one of her old business cards. She'd kept them just in case. As long as she was honest about not being on the force anymore it did not feel unethical to her. She handed the card to Gayle.

"I believe the young woman they found was staying in the room next to us at the Cliff's Edge, and I was hoping to talk to Sheriff McBride about it."

Gayle took the business card and examined it. She knew anyone could print any business card they wanted to and present themselves as someone they were not. She handed the card back to Linda and said, "Let me speak to him. Take a seat, please."

There were two long, narrow padded benches along the left wall. Linda and Kirsten walked over and sat down. When they were out of earshot, Gayle put on a headset, pushed a button on her phone, and immediately started talking.

Linda couldn't hear what Gayle was saying. She had no idea if they would succeed, or if they would be denied access to the sheriff. Gayle finished her conversation and said nothing, returning to work on her desk.

"Well?" Kirsten asked. "What do you think happened?"

The answer came not from Linda or from Gayle, but from the entrance moments later of Sheriff Jon McBride. He was, by Linda's judgment, a very handsome man. He stood well over six feet, with a gray crew cut, gym physique, large thighs (the sort of thing Linda noticed), hands to match, and a gun on his hip. His brown uniform was as crisp as his manner as he walked up to them and introduced himself.

"Jon McBride," he said, offering his hand.

Linda and Kirsten stood at the same time.

"Linda Sikorsky, and this is Kirsten McClellan."

Linda noticed a ring on McBride's left hand. Would he have worn one just a few years ago? Or had he been out all his career—something she doubted but did not assume—and being a married gay sheriff in small town Maine just wasn't what it used to be?

"I understand you have information for me," he said.

"I'm not sure if we do, that's the truth of it," she said. "But I'm almost certain Cayley Drees was at the Cliff's Edge last night, in the room next to ours."

McBride looked them over so quickly it would be missed by someone less attentive than Linda: he knows, she thought. We're more than friends, and he doesn't care.

"So tell me what you think," he said.

"Here? In the lobby?" asked Kirsten

"We don't call it a lobby," said McBride. "And don't worry. Gayle there never repeats anything she's heard, unless it's to me."

No-nonsense and direct, thought Linda. She knew she would have to be the same.

"I heard her being killed," she said.

Kirsten stared at her. This was not something Linda had told her.

"Or maybe it was the aftermath," Linda clarified. "*Something* happening to her in the middle of the night. Then I heard a car trunk shutting, and the car pulling out. I'm sorry to just show up like this ..."

"Lucille Proctor told me you were coming," he said. "Now I think we should go into my office."

He led them past Gayle and headed down the corridor to her right.

"No metal detectors?" Linda asked, surprised at the openness of the sheriff's office.

McBride smiled slightly as they walked down the hallway. "Gayle's our metal detector, and she shoots to kill."

Linda did not doubt him. They followed him past two rooms she pegged as interrogation rooms, a copy room with files, and a small pantry for coffee that had a vending machine in it. She remembered what it was like working with her fellow cops, the smells, sounds and camaraderie, and she missed it, but only for a moment. The past was not a place she spent much time these days. She'd lived in it all her life with the death of her father, wondering what slight change could have made their lives turn out differently. But the past cannot be changed, and dwelling in it only made the present pass unnoticed. They reached his office, as crisp and sparse as the man who occupied it, and took the two chairs in front of his desk as he closed the door behind them.

15

TREVOR WILCOX

THE PAST is never more than a memory away, as Daniel Wiley knew too well. He'd spent the last twenty years attempting to outrun things he had seen and done, but the night sweats that still came upon him from time to time, and the dreams that hovered like ghosts just beyond the line of consciousness, would not let him. He had only pretended to be someone else, to imagine success at burying Trevor Wilcox. Then a dream came, or a name appeared in something he read, and he went from being Daniel to being Trevor again.

Disappearing is not an easy thing to do. Now that everyone put photos of themselves online and surrendered to a culture of narcissism and constant sharing, usually with hundreds of disinterested pseudo-friends, it was nearly impossible. He'd made his run two decades ago, before Facebook and Twitter, before the internet was much more than listservs and email. He'd managed to avoid most of it, except having an email under his new name. Other than that, he was not on social media and never would be. He feared that someone, somehow, would see his face and recognize him. He had not gone far. He had hidden in plain view for the most part, but he had hidden well. When he got on that bus twenty years ago, taking nothing with him but a wad of cash and the few crucial items of a new identity that had taken him months and great expense to acquire, he had intended to leave Trevor Wilcox standing by the road where the bus picked up travelers. It worked. When he got off the bus, he was Daniel Wiley. A man with no past but the one he'd invented. An orphan and an only child, willing to do whatever work he could find. Fate, which had been so unkind to him, had finally smiled on his small life. He became another man, a man with nothing to conceal or reveal. A quiet man who minded his own business, had no relationships, sought the company of no one.

Daniel (for he no longer thought of himself as Trevor, even in the privacy of his mind) had seen the reporter's death on the news. Webley County was two hours from Ogunquit and Lonesome Pointe was a world away, but the tragic murder of a young journalist made news around the state. She had since been identified. Daniel was following the story online and already there was speculation about a connection between what she did for a living and how she died. Surely no one would kill a reporter for saying something negative about a local restaurant, or misspelling the name of an award winning cheerleader. No, that's preposterous. Big city reporters got themselves killed in far off lands, or kidnapped and beheaded in the desert. There could be no connection but the one made by capricious fate, all those wrong places at the wrong times. So the public thought, so they tweeted. But Daniel knew better. Daniel knew his phone call to Cayley Drees had set into motion a chain of events that led directly to that roadside, to that field where her body was discovered.

He also knew of another connection no one had made, a turning point that changed everything: the Cliff's Edge. He'd been set to meet Cayley there and tell her the full story of his life, of Trevor Wilcox—what he remembered, the actions he had taken and the crushing silence they had demanded. He'd planned to go through with it, too, but danger still waited in Lonesome Pointe. Had he gone there, had he not called first and been told the Drees woman had not checked in, his might be the body on the side of the road. He'd tried to reach her cell phone but no one answered. It had made him suspicious. Was this a trap? Was she bringing someone else? Why didn't she answer her phone? It had not occurred to him that cell reception was spotty during a storm, or that the front desk clerk had lied to him.

He cursed himself for avoiding her the last two days. She'd had no way of contacting him—that was the condition he set when they first began talking. *He* would call *her*, always from a pay phone. They still existed if you knew where to find them, and he knew of three within a half-hour's drive. He'd used them in rotation, like some spy on a TV show. He was terrified she would figure out that Daniel Wiley was her source; and from there that Daniel Wiley had once been Trevor Wilcox, and that Trevor Wilcox had once done a very, very bad thing. This was something he would tell her face-to-face.

The universe is a kind of fabric. He was beginning to understand that as he aged. Absolutely everything was connected; the connections were just not visible to the human eye, or the human mind. An anonymous phone call leads to the death of a woman whose only mistake was answering the phone. A child's afternoon gone wrong leads to a man's life on the run, if creating a new identity can be called running. In fact, Daniel had not run since the day he stepped off the bus in Ogunquit. He'd gotten on in Lonesome Pointe as Trevor Wilcox, gotten off as Daniel Wiley and never run again, except from the truth of it all. From that he had been running nearly his entire life.

It had to stop. What was unknown had to become known. Justice had to prevail somehow, even if it meant his ruin.

You're a coward, Trevor, he thought. Hearing his real name, spoken by his own mind-voice, shocked him. *Trevor, Trevor, Trevor.*

The time to be Trevor again had come at last. There was no running now, no hiding. He had to step into daylight, to risk everything he thought precious in exchange for setting the world right again. She had family, this Cayley Drees. She had loved ones and friends and co-workers. She deserved better than to pay the price for his wickedness, and she would have it.

Trevor would go to Lonesome Point. He would go to the Cliff's Edge. He would find people to listen, now that the one woman who had was dead. He would suffer, if that was required of him. And when it was all said and done, he would find peace.

He took his wallet filled with identification for a man named Daniel Wiley. He threw an extra shirt, a pair of underwear and socks, into his backpack. He looked around his small apartment where he had lived for nearly twenty years above the tobacconist's shop. Would he see it again? Was he entitled to, given the damage he'd done? It didn't matter. What mattered was coming out from under the heavy, heavy burden of his secrets. Some people would be relieved, and some would want him dead. It was a risk he had to take.

He locked the door behind him, headed down the narrow stairs to the street and around back where his car was parked. Two minutes later he was driving down the highway, headed to a place in the fabric of the universe where he'd torn it all those years ago, wanting only to make it whole again. He did not expect to return.

16

SHERIFF MCBRIDE

SHERIFF JON McBride had held his office for the past three years, being duly elected by the good people of Webley County and a few bad ones. He never asked the latter if they'd voted for him when he eased them into the back of his patrol car, arresting them for everything from petty theft to public drunkenness. He'd been with the Sheriff's Department for thirteen years since making a career transition from car salesman in his late 20s. Sales just wasn't in his blood the way it was in his father's and his brother Sam's. Emmett McBride still had his car lot in Wathingham and he still sold cars at the age of seventy-three, but mostly he hovered in the showroom pretending to be important and enjoying the deference shown to him by Sam and the other staff. He'd been disappointed when Jon left to join law enforcement, not least because he worried about his youngest son. Cops got killed, and even though it had not happened once in the county's history, it could. It was the *could* that kept Emmett up at night when Jon was called out on some emergency. It was the *could* that made him insist Jon phone home every evening of his life. His wife—Jon's mother—had passed away ten years ago, and old Emmett lived alone now, determined to stay in his own home until they carried him out on a mortician's gurney.

Linda and Kirsten sat in front of McBride's desk waiting for him to say something. Once he'd sat down, he'd started rifling through papers on his desk, then turned to his computer and finished writing an email. Linda did not know if this was part of his technique, or if he was just busy when they showed up.

Linda took the opportunity to glance discreetly around the room. No photographs, much like Lucille Proctor's office had looked. There were commendations on the wall, and a plaque recognizing someone for something—she assumed it was the sheriff or his department, but for all she knew it could have been an honor for his child, if he had one.

"So," McBride said at last. "You think this young woman was killed in the room next to you at the Cliff's Edge."

"I can't say for sure," said Linda.

"It's a very serious thing to speculate. Why would you?"

"Because I heard something, at around three o'clock this morning."

He looked at Kirsten, who said, "I was asleep. I didn't hear anything. But I know Linda, and when she says she heard something, she heard something."

"You're a cop?" he asked.

"Retired. I was on the New Hope force for twenty years, a homicide detective for the last six."

"And you think this gives you some special power, some insight into bumps you hear in the night?"

Linda blushed. She worried she was not being believed. Why would he believe her? What *had* she heard, exactly, and why would she think it was a murder?

"I know just a few things," Linda said. "There was a car in the parking spot in front of room six, next to ours."

"You were in five?"

"Seven. We were in room seven. There was a gold Camry, at least I'm very sure that's what it was. We—I—didn't hear anything during the evening, after we came back from eating at Marge's Diner. We went to sleep …"

"Go on."

"Then I had a bad dream. I woke up, and that's when I heard a noise in the next room."

"A struggle?"

"Not exactly."

"So again, why would you think an assault was being committed?"

Linda was getting frustrated. She wondered if they had wasted their time coming here.

"Instinct," she said, hoping it might resonate with the sheriff. The rest of the world might think instinct was hooey, but cops knew it well and were saved by it many times.

"I just had a clear suspicion something bad had happened. Then I heard the door open." Had she? She wasn't sure about that part, but she must have heard the door open. "Then I heard the sound of a car trunk being shut."

"Slammed?"

"No, just shut. I know the sound, I shut ours often enough. And then the car drove off."

McBride waited for more. After Linda did not continue, he said, "This sounds like someone hitting the road very early, that's all. The noise was probably a suitcase dropping on the floor. The trunk sound was the suitcase being put there. And the driving away sound is pretty self-explanatory. You can't very well leave if you don't drive away."

"Then why did the desk clerk say no one was in the room?" Kirsten said.

"Excuse me?"

"The guy at the front desk, the creepy one, he said the room was empty."

"You asked him?"

"We did," said Linda. "He said the room had been empty for a week after some couple trashed it."

"He said he hadn't gotten around to cleaning it up," Kirsten added.

This got McBride's attention. He knew Lenny Winfrow. Lenny had spent considerable time in the back of the sheriff's patrol cars. Minor drug use, two-bit crime and one sexual assault for which the charges had been dropped. Lenny was bad news. Hearing that he'd lied about someone staying at the Cliff's Edge—for McBride did not doubt this part of the women's story—raised a red flag for him.

Just then a deputy opened the door and entered carrying a file. Short, blond, formal in his manner and very well-built, Linda guessed him to be in his mid-to-late thirties. He looked at the women briefly, then placed the file on McBride's desk. Something very subtle passed between the men, and Linda quickly looked at his left hand: a ring matching the one McBride wore. *Interesting*, Linda thought. A gay sheriff married to one of his deputies. She suddenly liked Maine, *a lot*.

The deputy left the room. McBride gave no indication he cared what they thought or would reveal anything.

"We're just beginning to investigate the death," he said. "We can't say it was a homicide at this point. And anything we can say I won't tell you."

"Understood," said Linda.

"Will you go to the Cliff's Edge and talk to this guy?" asked Kirsten.

"I'd say there's a high probability of that."

Linda sensed their time was running out. They'd come here and told a very short story, and now they would be leaving. She needed more, *something*, to keep the visit from being a bust.

"What can you tell me about the Cliff's Edge?" she asked.

McBride looked at her—he wasn't expecting this. He frowned a moment, thinking, then said, "It's a strange place."

"How so?" said Linda. "What makes it strange?"

"Its history," he said, as if it were common knowledge, which it probably was in Lonesome Pointe. "It was before my time. I was very young when the property changed hands. *Very young*, like two years old. All I know is what I heard later, when I was old enough to understand what people said."

"What did they say?" asked Kirsten. She was sitting up now, and Linda knew her wife's curiosity had been sparked.

"They said the place was haunted. That the old woman who sold Russell Drover the property suddenly vanished. They said he killed her for it and buried her on the land. We were told to stay away from the Cliff's Edge, all the kids were. Considering what a son of a bitch Drover was, it wasn't hard to obey that order."

"Was it always a motel?" Linda asked.

"Once it was built, yes," said McBride. "That was really behind the stories, I think. People wanted it torn down. The place has been an eyesore for years. I don't know when it was first constructed, but the neighbors, such as they are out there—maybe I should say the townspeople—they wanted it gone. Claire Lindstrom, I think that was the original owner's name, she didn't vanish. She got the place off her hands just about when it should have been demolished, then she left town."

"You know this?" said Kirsten.

"I don't know it, and I don't much care. But nobody got killed, and there are no ghosts out there. Just a rickety piece-of-crap motel everybody wished was gone. And they still do."

"I understand Russell Drover committed suicide a few months back," Linda said.

McBride stared at her. She'd been in town for less than twenty-four hours and already she knew about Russell Drover's untimely demise.

"I was told that when we went to the All Pointes Bulletin office," Linda explained. "I was also told Cayley Drees had been contacted by someone about the death, or at least the obituary. Three months later she's found dead in a field, whether she stayed at the Cliff's Edge or not."

"Why would she stay there?" McBride asked. "Wathingham isn't even two hours away.

"Maybe she was returning to the scene of the crime," Kirsten offered.

"'Returning' implies she'd been there when the crime was committed," said McBride. "It also implies there *was* a crime. Drover's death was ruled a suicide and I have no reason to doubt that."

"Somebody doubted it," Kirsten said.

Linda wished Kirsten would stop talking. She could alienate the sheriff by suggesting he had not done his job well enough to know a suicide from a homicide.

"I'm sure your medical examiner is highly qualified," Linda said, "and if he believes it was a suicide ..."

"She."

"She, if she ruled it a suicide, I'm sure it was. But someone thought otherwise, and that someone may have lured Cayley Dress to the motel."

"Lured?"

"Or arranged to meet, or *something*. They got Cayley to go there, and things went wrong."

"Is this how you worked on the New Hope police force?" McBride asked. It was a cutting question. Instinct was one thing, fantasy another. Linda could tell he thought she was relying too much on conjecture.

"I don't mean any disrespect, Ms. Sikorsky," he said. "But you seem to be filling in a lot of blanks, and doing it in a way that will lead you to your foregone conclusion: that someone murdered Russell Drover, and then Cayley Drees. The same someone? Different someones? What else would you like to fantasize?"

Linda knew it was time to go. They'd done what they came here to do. They'd alerted the sheriff to something strange and probably criminal taking place at the Cliff's Edge the night before. There was nothing left to do. Linda did not want to further annoy a sheriff she might need to talk to again before they left town.

"What did you say the woman's name was, the one who sold the motel to Russell Drover?" she asked.

"Claire Lindstrom," he said. He slid his chair back, standing to see them out.

"Is there a library in town?" Linda asked.

"Town's not big enough for a library. Are you in need of a book?"

"No," Linda said, getting up from her chair. "I just wanted to see … take a look back at the town's history."

"You mean the history of the Cliff's Edge."

"Well, yes. That too."

"There's this thing called the internet," he said, and this time he smiled. "But you might not find anything from that long ago. I'm telling you, though, the Cliff's Edge isn't haunted. Russell Drover killed himself, it's not uncommon for the elderly to check out when they think the time's come. And Claire Lindstrom was not murdered for her scrap of land or her rundown roadside motel."

McBride came around his desk and was about to open to door to escort them out.

"Why is the motel still in operation after Drover's death?" Linda asked.

That stopped him. With his hand on the door handle, he said, "Because his daughter took it over, that's why."

"I didn't know he had a daughter."

"Why would you?"

"No reason, it's just new information, that's all. What's her name?"

"Dolores Drover," McBride said. "Now I really have to get back to work. I'll look into this business at the Cliff's Edge. Mostly because it's hinky that Lenny Winfrow said the room's been empty for a week. Rooms mean money. Empty ones don't make any. Doesn't make much sense, if that's what he said."

Linda heard the *if* and knew McBride might be thinking they'd embellished their story. He might even think they'd lied, which would shame anyone as honest as Linda Sikorsky. But she had no control over what he thought of them, and she had an hour's less time now that they'd come here.

Two minutes later they were back at the car, having made it safely past Gayle and whatever gun she kept within arm's reach.

"Where to now?" Kirsten asked as she buckled her seatbelt.

"Back to Marge's Diner," Linda said.

"But I'm not hungry."

"Neither am I. Didn't you see the sign?"

"What sign?"

"The misspelled one that said 'We Have WhyFi.' We're going to order some coffee, and maybe some pie so they'll let us sit there awhile, and we're going to make use of your laptop. As Sheriff McBride just told us, there's this thing called the internet."

Linda buckled up, started the car and headed to the next corner to circle back. She was not about to make an illegal U-turn in front of the Sheriff's Department and find herself delayed by a ticket.

17

DOLORES DROVER

DOLORES DROVER spent twenty years estranged from her father before she came back to kill him—or have him killed, which was the case. She doubted the law would think there was much difference between the two; she would go to prison for the rest of her life if they were caught, but they would not be. Meredith was too smart for that. Meredith lived in a state of control over her environment and the people in it, including Dolores, but Dolores didn't mind. They were lovers, in love, housed in a state of love, surrounded by and immersed in love. They had only been together physically for nine months, but their hearts had been connected since Dolores first recognized her feelings for Meredith in high school. Dolores was only a freshman then while Meredith was a senior. The age difference added to the allure. It made Meredith seem that much more unattainable. And when they had kissed that first time, when Meredith had acknowledge Dolores's interest and given her the greatest gift of her young life—an embrace and a kiss from a goddess—the memory of it settled into Dolores's mind and heart and sat there like a burning ember for thirty-five years. Then one day, alone in her small efficiency apartment in Bangor, a card arrived with a letter inside. Out of the blue and as charged as a thunderbolt. Meredith Vesey remembered her. Meredith confessed her love after all these years. Meredith, too, had suffered with a longing, lived with it inside her, nagging at her, whispering to her, finally consuming her until she had to reach out, she had to hope. Did Dolores remember, she asked? Did Dolores recall that kiss, that flood of joy? Was happiness together still a possibility for them?

Dolores drove to Lonesome Pointe the next day, taking a half-full suitcase and leaving the rest for her landlord to throw away when he realized she wasn't coming back. She possessed very little, and wanted even less. What she wanted least of all was to reconnect with her bastard father, the one who'd told her twenty years ago to find a good man and pop out some grandkids, "Or else." Russell Drover didn't hate gay people—they were paying customers, too, from time to time, especially the married men with wives who didn't know their old men were sucking each other off in one of the motel rooms—but he didn't like having one for a daughter. A chubby, lazy, dull child who to his mind had never accomplished anything and wasn't good for more than housekeeping, of which she did a poor job. Their mutual animosity reached a boiling point one Saturday afternoon. Russell was lecturing her again on the finer points of delousing sheets after unsavory guests had slept in them ("sleep" being the usual euphemism for screwing), when her attention strayed and he yelled at her.

"You ain't got much of a mind to wander," he'd said. "Keep it focused, girl."

She had stared at him a moment, the fury from a lifetime of abuse and ridicule roaring through her blood, and she slapped him. And slapped him again.

He'd stood there dumbfounded. What was this? Who was this person hitting him? He was the one who did the hitting, and when it was clear he was about to start doing that, Dolores turned her back on him. She walked out of the Cliff's Edge with only her raggedy purse, her raggedy shoes and her tattered self-esteem, and she never came back.

Until the card with the letter arrived. Until she knew love was possible even for her.

So it came as quite a surprise, a shock even, when Meredith asked her to mend fences with the old coot. Russell Drover was looking for a buyer for the motel and willing to sell to just about anyone but Meredith Vesey. She'd kept upping her offer, well past what the property was worth, but still he wouldn't sell to her. He didn't like Meredith Vesey. Hated her, in fact. He told Lenny Winfrow, another longtime paid source for Meredith (one can learn many valuable secrets from a motel front desk clerk) that he would sell to the Devil himself before he'd sell to Meredith Vesey. It left her with few options until she remembered the kiss with his estranged daughter and she woke one morning with a plan.

Dolores would do anything Meredith asked. Meredith told her they had a chance to own their own motel, to fix it up and make it what it always could have been. People would want to stay there. They would get 5-star reviews online. Travel websites would list them as a must-stay destination. All they had to do was own it! Russell wouldn't sell it to her, though, and that made Meredith's dream just about impossible, unless …

Dolores had listened to Meredith's plan as they sipped a special wine Meredith said she'd saved all these years hoping this moment would come. Dolores didn't know anything about wine, but Meredith said this was very expensive and rare. It looked like wine Dolores had seen in a cooler at the QuickMart, but Meredith assured her it was from France and only people like George Clooney and Ellen DeGeneres could afford it. Dolores did not doubt her. Dolores let herself be cradled in Meredith's arms and listened as Meredith asked her to reconcile with her father. He was old, he was looking to retire (to where she did not know or care). Surely he would rather leave the motel to his daughter and see it continue, if only they were on speaking terms.

Dolores set about doing as Meredith asked. She could barely sleep, thinking of what they would do with the Cliff's Edge and how amazing their life would be there. All she had to do was take that first step, make that first visit. And never, ever, let him know his daughter had come back for Meredith Vesey and not for him.

It had not taken long. Even a son of a bitch like Russell Drover had a heart somewhere inside him. He'd missed his daughter. He had never been able to find good help, and she was very good when she returned. She did not have to be taught how to properly clean a room. It was as if she'd been practicing twenty years for this. He had even offered her one of the rooms to live in, but she'd told him she had a place in town—which was true, a place secured for her with utmost secrecy by Meredith, who stressed they could not live together, not yet—and after two months she asked him about his will. So relieved was he to have his wayward daughter back (he did not harp on grandchildren now, since Dolores was too old in his opinion to be good for mothering), that instead of being suspicious he went and finally made a will. He'd never had one before. Apparently Russell Drover expected to live forever, or at least to die broke.

His expectations were wrong on both counts.

* * *

"I have ears everywhere," Meredith said, her arm resting on

Dolores's as they sat in the sun room. Dolores had made them raspberry tea, Meredith's favorite. "Except in the sheriff's office. Believe me, I've tried. But nothing gets past that old battleax Gayle. She'd know if there was a mole in the place and she'd shoot it dead, then drop it on McBride's desk."

"No doubt about it," said Dolores. She was thrilled when their arms touched; it gave her comfort in a world that had offered her none. "So what are we gonna do?"

"I'm still thinking that through."

Meredith had spent some time researching the retired detective from New Hope after Lenny Winfrow told her the two women were snooping. She'd been sure they were a couple, then confirmed it when she read about Linda Sikorsky's second-hand store—for what else could you call it?—and, most importantly, her years with the police force. As a homicide detective, no less. The more she read, the more alarmed she became. There was an article online about her solving a murder at Pride Lodge, whatever the hell that was. A gay resort? Why did they still exist? It didn't matter to her, she would never go there. She learned about the ex-detective's involvement in ending the career of the Pride Killer: New York City's most famous serial killer halted in his tracks by none other than Linda Sikorsky and some guy named Kyle Callahan. The word "dogged" came to mind, her worries growing with her knowledge of the woman now coming after her. For that is surely what was happening. Linda Sikorsky had caught a scent and was slowly coming up behind Meredith, her nose to the ground. Was she armed? Meredith had to assume so. Was she dangerous? Absolutely. Would she succeed? Never.

"Maybe we should kill Jeb Harris," Dolores said, referring to the retired reporter whose story had brought up memories no one wanted.

Her matter-of-fact tone chilled Meredith. She had manipulated the idiot well and easily, but sometimes she worried that Dolores was too cold inside, the kind of cold that enjoyed ending people's lives, or at least telling other people to do it. She'd known since Russell Drover's death—which they had confirmed by seeing his body with a hole blown through its chest—that Dolores took pleasure in gruesome things. Her years alone, resenting to the point of pure hatred, had made her indifferent to suffering. She put on a good front, and she certainly loved Meredith with an irrational exuberance, like a puppy brought in from the cold and fed every time it yapped. But there was something not right about her. Meredith was keenly aware of this and knew the time might come when Dolores turned on her. It happens.

"He's in Florida," said Meredith. "He's no concern of ours. This Sikorsky bitch is not about to take a side trip to Coral Springs just to track down a story that didn't really say anything. Rumor, conjecture, gossip. It was a silly story more about a haunting and Claire Lindstrom's sudden disappearance. Stupid, small town nonsense."

"Nonsense," Dolores repeated. It was a habit Meredith disliked among many.

Meredith knew that no one, not Jeb Harris or Sheriff McBride or Cayley Drees, would come anywhere near the truth of it all. Only one person knew that, and he'd been gone many years now. She had tried to find him, but for someone as hapless and pliable as Trevor Wilcox, he had done a superb job of vanishing from the face of the earth. At least until he'd made the mistake of contacting Cayley Drees. Meredith could not be certain it was him, but she had deduced it once Drees started asking questions. The young woman had not been as good a reporter as she'd imagined herself to be. A call to the Cliff's Edge, a second call to Dolores herself. Understandable mistakes for someone pursuing a story, but helpful to Meredith's cause. She had seen the reporter coming long before Cayley Drees had any hope of seeing Meredith and what Meredith had in store for her.

She knew Drees had come to the Cliff's Edge to meet someone, and she was sure that someone was Trevor Wilcox. Only that would explain the secrecy she knew about from Rudy at the All Pointes. He'd told Meredith about Drees's sneaking, the fact she'd kept whatever she was working on to herself. She had not told Lucille Proctor or anyone else about her contact with the anonymous caller. No one had known she was coming to the Cliff's Edge. Except her mysterious source, the one Meredith believed she'd gone there to meet. The one who'd called and been told by Lenny that no one named Cayley Drees had shown up and the storm was just about to hit.

"Where's Claire Lindstrom?" Meredith asked. She was talking to herself; there was no reason to think Dolores would know.

Surprising Meredith so much she nearly spit up her tea, Dolores said, "Big View trailer park, outside Wells."

"Excuse me?"

"They don't call them trailer parks anymore. Big View Mobile Estates, I think it is."

"And how do you know this, My Sweet?"

"We kept in touch. Letters. She don't own a computer."

Well, well, well, thought Meredith. The original owner of the Cliff's Edge, whom so many people liked to imagine had suddenly disappeared, had not gone very far. Wells was just an hour away.

"Why didn't you tell me?" Meredith asked.

"I didn't think it was important." Dolores looked worried, as if she'd peed on the carpet.

"Relax, Dolores, it's important but not in a bad way. You didn't do wrong."

She could see Dolores visibly relax.

"Do we have to kill her?" asked Dolores, frowning.

"What's with the killing everybody!" Meredith said. "I think you take too much pleasure in it, now that you've got a taste. It's not something to be done lightly, and never personally. These are all business decisions."

She had never told Dolores why she wanted the Cliff's Edge. She did not dare, for then Dolores would know she had been fooled and used. The time may come to inform her of that, but not yet.

"You have a phone number for old Claire? She must be about eighty by now."

"Last April," Dolores said. "The only time I saw her."

Jesus, thought Meredith. *This woman is full of surprises.*

"My car was in the shop so I took the bus to Wells and a taxi from there to Big View. We had a nice afternoon, some frosted muffins I took her, even had a birthday candle in one of them. She's very sweet and still got her mind at that age."

"She wasn't so goddamned sweet back then," Meredith said, immediately regretting it. Claire had not liked children, or maybe she just hadn't like Meredith.

Dolores looked stricken. "I'm sorry, I didn't know it mattered."

"How could you? Please, don't worry about it. I'd just like to talk to her, if you have a phone number. Or does she not have a phone either?"

"Oh, she's got a phone. She only answers it sometimes and we've spoken maybe twice over the years, but last time I called I got her voicemail, so it works."

"Let's try our luck, shall we?" Meredith said. "Fetch me my cell and we'll call Claire just to say hi, give her the good news about the Cliff's Edge."

"I'm not sure it'll be good news for her. She dumped the place on my father."

"What, did she think it was haunted, too?"

"I don't know, Meredith. She never said. I think she just wanted out. Running a motel's not easy."

Meredith decided it was time to stroke her pet again. "We're finding that out now, aren't we?" she said, skimming her fingers along Dolores's arm.

"When we gonna fix it up?" Dolores asked, slipping quickly into her fantasies of a luxury motel just off a busy highway. It was really going to be something.

"Soon," said Meredith. "But first we have to tie up all these loose ends, send this Sikorsky woman packing. Now let's make that phone call."

Dolores jumped up, kissed Meredith on the cheek, and hurried into the kitchen to get Meredith's cell phone. She'd plugged it in to charge after the call with Rudy. The battery would be full now, and the reception up here in Meredith's hill top home was exceptional.

18

MARGE'S DINER

BUSINESS AT Marge's slowed during the mid-afternoon hours. When Linda and Kirsten were there for breakfast they'd been lucky to find a parking spot. Now, with the lunch crowd gone and dinner several hours away, they had their pick. Linda counted a total of six cars in the lot and figured at least three of those belonged to people working there. She wondered which was Betsy's, then took a guess on the beat up yellow VW Beetle with the giant pink dice hanging from the rearview mirror. She could be wrong, but Betsy had seemed like the sort of woman who would have something big and pink dangling in her window.

She pulled into a slot near the diner's front door, next to a rusted pickup that had once been blue.

"What are we looking for, exactly?" Kirsten asked, grabbing her laptop from the back seat.

"I'll know when we find it," Linda replied. "I'd like to read over that story Jeb Harris wrote about the Cliff's Edge, that's a good start. Then let's see what else is out there in the vast data storehouse of the internet."

Linda locked the car and they headed inside. Betsy was still there and Linda recognized the cook through the kitchen window, as well as one helper when there had been two during breakfast. A young man was now working the cash register—so young that Linda guessed he was part of the owners' family, whoever they were.

"Back so soon?" Betsy said, heading toward them with a coffee pot in her hand. "You can ignore the 'Please Wait to be Seated' sign and just sit anywhere. You get your pick this time of day."

She was right. There were only five other people in the restaurant, two eating alone at two-tops and one group of three. All the other tables and booths were clean but empty.

Linda and Kirsten took a booth by the window. Kirsten always liked being able to see their car, even though there was nothing in it to steal and the car itself wouldn't fetch more than a few thousand dollars.

"Did you lock it?" Kirsten asked.

"Pointlessly so," said Linda.

She always locked the car—and the house, and anything else they owned that could be locked—and let it go at that. Worrying about someone stealing a belonging had never been a concern for her, excluding her guns, and those were stored in a safe, with the exception of her father's pistol that she kept in the bedroom and that was now in the car trunk. Even if someone stole the car they would not get into the gun case. Kirsten didn't like Linda traveling with a firearm, but Linda was licensed to do so as a retired police officer. She also had an unfortunate history of run-ins with murderers, so Kirsten decided it was best to get used to it. In fact, Linda was getting very close to convincing Kirsten to take up shooting. Now that Kirsten was writing a mystery series about a lesbian private detective, she'd warmed to the idea, "for research," she said. Linda knew once Kirsten learned to properly use and handle a gun, she would be hooked. There was a gun club not far from the house. The Horse Road Gun Club was, as Linda said, good people, and several of its members had become friends. You have to have friends living in the woods.

"I hope the battery's charged," Linda said, watching as Kirsten took the laptop out of its case.

"I always have it on a full charge, just in case."

Betsy came over with two menus and handed them to the women.

"Just coffee and toast, if that's okay," Linda said.

Betsy smiled, looking around the empty diner. "For now, but I may have to ask you to move when the rush comes."

"The rush?" said Kirsten.

"She's kidding," Linda said. "Isn't that right, Betsy?"

"You never know with me. So two coffees, two toasts. What kind of bread?"

Both women asked for whole wheat. Then Linda said, "Is there a password for the WiFi?"

"One guess."

"Betsy?"

"Bingo. You're as sharp as you look. Now settle in and enjoy yourselves. I'll let you know if there's a stampede coming." Kirsten turned on the laptop and connected to the internet while Linda glanced over the printed out story Rudy had given them. The coffee and toast arrived two minutes later, just as Kirsten pulled up Google and waited for Linda to tell her what they were searching for.

Kirsten waited, then waited some more while Linda read. She'd eaten half her toast when she finally cleared her throat to get Linda's attention.

"Just a minute, I'm almost finished," Linda said.

Kirsten decided to look up Serenity House again, the place they were supposed to be at that very moment. Not on the shore but close enough to see it, the famed bed and breakfast boasted three stories, with a variety of room sizes and styles on each floor. Ten years ago it was bought by a bibliophile and turned into a place for writers to come and relax while they wrote their next novel, or finished their last one. Kirsten had no idea how many of those guests actually published their books, or how many were even writers. But Serenity House had gained a reputation as a sort of authors' colony under one roof, and Kirsten was sure she would be able to finish her novel there. It had also, by some mysterious word of mouth, become popular with gay and lesbian authors, earning it an extra star in Kirsten's imaginary travel guide. She glanced at her watch, aware of the day passing and Linda's promise to be on the road by sundown.

"It's not all that revealing," Linda said at last, putting the article down. She sipped her coffee, which had gone nearly cold in the time it took to read the story.

"What's it say?"

"Just about the history of the Cliff's Edge, how it started as a general store a hundred years ago, then it got bought and torn down by someone named Claire Lindstrom. She put up a motel called the Seaview—why do they insist on picking names like that?—and how the town didn't want it there."

"I thought it was some kind of exposé," Kirsten said.

"In a small town way. It reads more like one of those local paper filler pieces. He talks about the rumors that Claire Lindstrom vanished—without any substantiation, by the way—and how people swore the place was haunted. He even spent a night there to see if any phantom maids showed up to clean the room with a blood soaked mop."

"It sounds like a dead end."

Linda thought about it a moment while she ate her cold toast.

"He does finish with something interesting," she said.

"And that would be?"

"He talks about Russell Drover wanting to sell the property."

"When did he buy it?"

"Forty years ago, from Claire Lindstrom. That was another thorn in the community's side. They didn't want a motel there in the first place and he kept it going."

"For forty years."

"That's right."

"So how is that interesting?"

Linda looked at her as if she should figure this out on her own. Kirsten was the mystery writer, after all.

"What would Rox Harmony make of it?" Linda asked.

Kirsten was surprised by the question. "Well ... he wants to sell the property forty years after he bought it, nothing suspicious there ..."

"Yes, keep going."

"And then, when he's trying to sell it, after Jeb's newspaper story ends, I assume, since you said he stopped there ..."

"Keep going."

"Suddenly a motel owner who wants to be free of the place, maybe go off to Florida or Arizona, somewhere welcoming to old bones ... kills himself."

"Precisely. Why would he do that when he was trying to sell the property?"

"Because he couldn't find a buyer?"

"That's a pretty flimsy excuse for suicide."

"Maybe he was depressed."

"Is that what Rox would think?"

"No," said Kirsten. "She would think he didn't kill himself. That someone didn't want the property sold, so they killed him and made it appear to be suicide."

"You're as sharp as you look," Linda said, repeating what Betsy had said to her.

"So," said Kirsten. "For the sake of argument and nothing concrete to go on, let's assume old Russell was killed to prevent him from selling. Who do we look at? What do we ask?"

"We start by finding out what happened to Claire Lindstrom. Why did she vanish? Where did she go, and why did she go there so quickly?"

"She could be dead. Forty years is a long time."

"So do a search. See if there's an obituary for her. Or if she's been seen at a charity function or she won a million dollars at a slot machine, anything."

"Right," Kirsten said, then she went to work searching online.

Five minutes later, looking frustrated, Kirsten said, "Nothing. Not a word."

Linda knew it was difficult for people to be completely unrecorded in some fashion on the internet. Even if they did not have Facebook pages or Twitter accounts, almost everyone was mentioned somewhere online. Newspapers now made digital archives of their back issues, often going back decades.

Betsy showed up at the table again, startling them both. They'd been lost in concentration and had not seen her approach the table with her coffee pot.

"You gals want a refill?" Betsy said.

"I'm fine," Linda said. "We'll get out of your way soon."

"No rush," said Betsy. "That stampede hasn't arrived yet."

She was about to leave them when Linda said, "Hey, Betsy ..."

"Yes?"

"You know anything about the history of the Cliff's Edge?"

"No, can't say I do, and can't say I want to. It's a dump, from what I hear. Terrible about Russell Drover, you know, the way he died, but it's not a place I've ever had any interest in knowing about."

"I hear the town never liked it, didn't want it there," Kirsten said.

"That's true enough. And they'll go on not liking it. His daughter runs the place now."

"Dolores," Kirsten said.

"That's right. It was the sweetest thing. Strange, but sweet. She left town when I was just out of high school, never saw her again until maybe six months ago. She came back. I'm guessing the old man left it to her."

"We didn't see her at the motel," Linda said.

"She doesn't live there, far as I know," Betsy said. Then she looked around, as if someone might overhear her. She knew many of the town's secrets, the skeletons kept in closets that were revealed in casual conversation at Marge's Diner. She prided herself on not gossiping and did not want to violate her own standards now.

"I hear she's got a place in Lonesome Pointe … and that she spends a lot of time with Meredith Vesey alone up at that house."

"*That* house?" Linda said.

"The Vesey place. Meredith Vesey is the only one left in that family and seems like she plans to die there. That's all I know, so let's leave it at that."

Meredith Vesey, another name new to Linda and Kirsten. She wanted to ask who this Meredith was and why Betsy had lowered her voice when she spoke about her. But it was evident Betsy did not want to cross this line any further, and Linda would not push, at least not on that subject.

"What about Claire Lindstrom?" Linda asked.

"Who?" said Betsy.

"Claire Lindstrom. She owned the motel when it was called the Seaview. She sold it to Drover, then disappeared."

"I don't know that name, sorry."

A voice came from across the aisle. "I do," it said.

They all turned to see an old woman sitting at a two-top having just finished what appeared to be chicken fried steak. She looked to be in her seventies, if not older, but thin, strong and perfectly alert. Linda knew immediately she had been listening to their conversation.

"She didn't disappear," the woman said. "She moved away in a hurry, that's all. People are free to do that in America."

Betsy said, "This is Grace Hinkley. Grace, these two ladies are from …"

"New Jersey," Linda said. "Passing through."

"It's an odd thing for someone to ask who's just passing through," said Grace. "But I know the rumors, and I know they're nonsense. Claire relocated, simple as that, and who can blame her? Lonesome Pointe's not exactly a tourist hotspot. Got one sad lighthouse you won't find in a travel guide. Got an eyesore of a motel outside of town, and we got Marge's Diner, with the best waitress in a hundred miles, maybe two."

Betsy smiled. "I gotta get back," she said. "The boss's son's on the cash register, he might tell his dad I spent a little too much time jawing with the customers. Just wave when you want the check."

Betsy walked off. Grace had turned slightly toward them, sliding her empty plate away.

"I know what happened to Claire because we stayed in touch."

This was very good news to Linda. "Do you still communicate?" she asked.

"Only through holiday cards," Grace said. "Neither one of us is much of a talker, least not on the phone. I don't think she even answers hers."

"Did she move out of state?" Kirsten asked.

Grace laughed. "Out of state? Hell, she didn't even leave the county. She's got a single wide over at the Big View Mobile Estates, about an hour from here. Fancy name for a trailer park, but she's there."

"Why did everyone think she vanished?" Kirsten said.

"Because she wanted them to!" Grace said, as if it was the most obvious answer in the world. "She hated it here. She tried to make a go of it with that motel, ended up near broke. Sold the place to Russell Drover and got the hell out of Dodge."

"It doesn't sound very mysterious," Linda said.

"It wasn't. But this is a small town. People need ghost stories and disappearing-person legends to tell themselves. Lucky for you you're just passing through."

"What keeps you here?" Kirsten asked.

"Look at me. I'm eighty-two years old. Bet you thought I was seventy, happens all the time. Got good genes. Considered leaving a hundred times myself but never did, and now it just doesn't seem worth it. It's not much of a place to be, but it's my place."

"Thank you for the information," Linda said.

"You find Claire, you tell her she missed Grace Hinkley's birthday. Not like her."

"We'll do that," Linda said. She waved at Betsy for the check. It was time to ask Claire Lindstrom a few questions.

They did not notice the beat-up Dodge Rambler sitting at the end of the parking lot. Had Linda seen the driver she would have recognized him, but he'd slid below the dashboard, his head up just enough to watch them leave the diner.

Lenny Winfrow had not had time to wait for Dolores to come back him up at the Cliff's Edge. Meredith had called and told him to find the women and follow them, now. He was not to worry about the motel. So he'd done what he often did since Russell Drover's demise: he put up the "Back in an Hour" sign, locked the office door and left. He might be back in twenty minutes, he might be back in three hours. It didn't matter and he didn't care. Things weren't looking so good for Meredith and Dolores, and if they were concerned, he had to be, too.

Lonesome Pointe and its surroundings were small enough that it didn't take much driving around before Lenny spotted Linda's car in the diner parking lot. He'd circled back, pulled in at the end of the lot—past the diner windows, close enough to the cigarette shop next door that he could be mistaken for a customer if anyone noticed, and he'd waited. He hated waiting.

Linda and Kirsten pulled away, having entered the Big View Mobile Estates into the car's GPS.

Following a safe distance behind was Lenny, enthusiastic murderer and go-to guy for all your criminal needs. Watching the women's car as he drove behind them just far enough to keep them in sight, he hoped Meredith would need his more lethal services again soon. It takes a certain self-awareness to know what you're good at and what you're not. Lenny was very good at putting a stop to things, and even better at putting a stop to people.

19

NO VACANCY

SHERIFF MCBRIDE had not been to the Cliff's Edge in several weeks, a break from the usual calls to deal with drunken motel guests and the occasional firing of a gun or violent altercation. He knew the place well, but preferred to see it from a distance, preferably as he drove by. There were good reasons the townspeople did not care for the old motel off the highway into town. It had been merely ugly and rundown when Claire Lindstrom owned it. Once Russell Drover took it over it became a way stop for the weary and lost, and, more significantly for a county sheriff, a place of ill repute where local youth and midlife crisis types rented rooms to act out their worst behaviors. Affairs were common at the Cliff's Edge, clandestine rendezvous with a best friend's wife or husband in various combinations. And while it was too far out of the way to be convenient for prostitution, at least one enterprising woman had rented a room for two months and conducted a brisk online business until one of her clients was robbed at gunpoint in the parking lot. By the time McBride got there the woman was long gone and the man declined to file a report, as married men caught with hookers often did.

Lenny Winfrow, too, had been the subject of Sheriff McBride's attention over the years. Lenny was suspected of dealing drugs with the Crimshaw brothers, who were themselves suspected of helping their grandmother to an early grave. (Nothing could be proved in that case; she'd broken her neck falling down her basement stairs, but McBride and most sensible people in town believed her grandsons had pushed her.)

McBride was expecting to see Lenny at the front desk when he arrived, but instead saw a sign on the door saying Winfrow would be back in an hour. The door was locked, and the sheriff stood staring through the front glass for a minute while he decided whether to head back to the station or kill an hour somehow and wait for Lenny's return.

He looked at the parking lot: there were only four cars there, for nine rooms. Counting Linda and Kirsten, that meant five rooms were empty. This included room #6, the one Sikorsky had said she'd heard noises from in the middle of the night. The one she swore she'd seen Cayley Drees's car parked in front of. He peered through the front door glass again, as if it might force Lenny to appear, then he decided to stroll along the rooms and see if anything seemed amiss.

As he passed the rooms he saw one man dressed for business who appeared to be preparing to leave. Fortunately for him there was a key slot in the front door for guests to leave their keys, just in case the stellar front desk clerk was gone for an hour or a half day. In another room he saw a couple just getting out of bed. The woman quickly ran to the window and closed the curtain.

Finally he came to room #6. The window drape was thick, dark and closed. He could see nothing inside. He tried peering in along the side of the curtain but saw only shadow. Wondering if he'd get lucky, he twisted the door handle. It was locked. He turned it several times anyway, hoping it was old and loose enough to give.

"May I help you, Sheriff?" a woman's voice said from behind him.

McBride jumped. Being surprised was a dangerous thing for a lawman. He kept his bearing and turned around.

Dolores Drover was standing behind him, staring at him with a smile that did not extend to her eyes.

McBride had never cared for the woman. She'd left town twenty years ago, which was not before his time. He was a grown man by then and still selling cars for his father. He knew, as all the town did, that Dolores and Russell did not get along, and when she left he'd expected to never see her again. Then she showed up, making nice with the old man and eventually inheriting the motel, which was, McBride figured, why she had come back in the first place. Nothing says kiss and make up like an estate, meager as it was.

"I was hoping to talk to Lenny," he said, looking past her to make sure no one else was about to surprise him.

"He's on an errand," Dolores said. "I just got here myself. Is there something I can help you with?"

McBride glanced around the lot. If Dolores had just gotten there he would have heard her car pull up.

Guessing what he was thinking, she said, "I parked around back. There's a carport there, maybe you forgot."

There was indeed a carport in back of the motel. Russell Drover had kept his old station wagon there. Still, she could not have just arrived or he would have seen and heard her.

"I've had a report of some suspicious activity," said McBride.

"At the Cliff's Edge? I don't think so, Sheriff. It could be local kids pulling a prank again."

"Yes, well, that's possible. But I'd like to have a look-see anyway, if you don't mind."

"And where would you like to have that look-see? I can let you into the office, but not into Lenny's room, that wouldn't be right."

"Actually," said McBride, looking at the door to room #6, "I'd like to have a look in this room."

Dolores kept smiling and staring. Without hesitation, she took a key ring from the pocket of her smock. One of the keys was a master that opened every door lock at the motel.

"Certainly," she said. "But don't mind the ammonia smell. I just cleaned it. Had a rowdy couple here last week and they made a terrible mess of the place. I finally got around to cleaning it up this morning."

So you just arrived, but you cleaned this room, McBride thought. *The timeline's looking a little shaky, Dolores.*

"I don't suppose you had the carpet replaced this morning, too?"

"Why would I do that?" she said, opening the door. "Carpets cost good money. Shampoo works just fine. Did have to burn the sheets, though."

"Was that before or after you just arrived?"

"Stripped the bed awhile back," she said, ignoring his jab. "Haven't been here long enough to burn any sheets, but you know that, Sheriff. Are you pulling my leg?"

He didn't want to pull her leg or any other part of her. His impression of Dolores Drover as a strange one had only intensified since her return to town. She'd been seen with Meredith Vesey many times, but everything was rumor when it came to Meredith and had been for years. Were the women having an affair? Did their relationship include the Cliff's Edge in some way? He had no time to think about it now and he would not ask Dolores, knowing she would only distort the facts or outright lie.

They entered room #6, Dolores going in first and standing by the door with her hand on the knob. She apparently thought this would not take long.

McBride looked at the room. He quickly stepped to the curtain and opened it, allowing daylight to poor in. What he saw discouraged him: the room had been stripped bare. The mattress had no sheets. Even the pillows were gone. There was no decoration of any kind to the room, no Georgia O'Keefe print on the wall, no fixtures. The dresser was bare and empty, which McBride discovered when he walked to it and pulled out the drawers. There was a television that looked thirty years old and broken on a stand across from the bed. The phone jack was disconnected from the wall.

Realizing he was going to take more than a quick glance around, Dolores let the door close. McBride looked up at the sound, as if being alone in the room with her was not a welcome situation.

He walked into the bathroom and was hit by the smell of bleach, ammonia and possibly some abrasive cleanser: everything had been washed, scrubbed, wiped down. The shower curtain was missing.

"What the hell did those people do in here?" he asked.

"I dread to think," said Dolores. "Some kind of sex party. I can't even tell you all the stuff we found, it's embarrassing, Sheriff, downright shameful."

"And what did you do with all this 'stuff?'"

"Threw that out a few days ago."

"Shower curtain. Sheets. Carpet shampoo. You want me to have a talk with these people? You must have them in your registry."

She waited a moment, then said, "We don't keep a guest list, if that's what you mean. Those days are long gone. I thought you'd know that, Sheriff McBride. Hotels don't make people sign a registry anymore."

"Is this a hotel now?" he said, smiling at her.

"It will be, when we fix it up."

McBride was standing by the bed now. "Who is 'we?'"

Her face hardened. "Me and Lenny, that's who. There isn't anybody else. I'm likely to hire a few, when the time comes. The Cliff's Edge is going to be a destination hotel."

"Motel."

"Call it whatever suits you, Sheriff. I've got plans for the place, and you'll likely want to stay here yourself, that's how nice it'll be. You and your husband."

"We have a home in town," McBride said. He was not pleased

with whatever message Dolores was trying to send him. There was no other reason for her to bring up Paul except to let him know she was aware of his private life. Everyone in town was; Jon and Paul had been together and open about their lives from the beginning. Still, there was a slight tone of menace in the way she'd said it.

"We could take a look at your credit card receipts, track this couple down that way," he said.

"They paid cash," Dolores replied. She opened the door: the visit from the prying Sheriff was over. "Most people pay cash here, but that'll change ..."

"When it's the preferred place to stay," he said, smiling.

"That's right."

They walked back outside. Dolores closed the door and checked the knob, making sure it had locked.

"So nobody stayed in this room last night?" McBride asked.

"Wasn't possible," she said.

"I'd like to ask Lenny some questions about that."

"He'll tell you the same."

"I'm sure he will. But I'd still like to talk to him. You think he'll be back soon?"

"Tell you what, Sheriff, I'll give him a call on his cell phone, tell him you were here and he should get in touch with you, how's that?"

"I'd appreciate that, Dolores." He started to walk away, then stopped. "How come you don't work the front desk when he's gone? Might lose a customer with nobody to take their cash."

"I'm not my father, greedy for every penny," Dolores said. "I own the Cliff's Edge now. Owners do some things, front desk help does others. Besides, I just got here, remember?"

"That's right. Anyway, you tell Lenny I'll be back. I heard that reporter may have stopped here yesterday."

"Reporter?"

"The one they found dead off the road this morning."

"I saw something about that on the news," Dolores said. "Such a tragedy. Can't imagine why she'd stop here in the storm we had, but you can ask Lenny about that. It just doesn't make much sense. Now if you'll excuse me, I need to get back to town, got some banking and whatnot to do."

McBride watched her walk around the back of the motel. He got into his patrol car and started the engine, waiting until he saw

Dolores Drover pull around front and drive out onto the highway. He was sure she would be watching him in her rearview mirror, waiting to make sure he left, too.

Something—many things, perhaps—was not right at the Cliff's Edge. Sheriff Jon McBride had the feeling he'd been told the truth by Linda Sikorsky, or at least what she imagined the truth to be. Something had happened in room #6, and it did not involve sex toys and bodily fluids of the pleasurable type. He had no grounds for a warrant, but that could change. For now he had a murder investigation to get back to.

He drove out and headed to the station, close enough to see Dolores's car in the distance.

Dolores watched McBride driving behind her. Was he following her? It didn't matter. She would stop at the bank, just like she'd told him. She would stay calm. And she would call Meredith as soon as she was sure Sheriff Jon McBride could not possibly see her.

20

BIG VIEW ESTATES

THE ONLY view offered at Big View Mobile Estates was of the other mobile homes on the property. It was a flat parcel of land Linda estimated to be no more than a half dozen acres, with perhaps fifty trailers secured to the ground and dressed in various forms of disguise—some with small fences, some with skirts, none with visible wheels. Mobile homes were obvious at a glance, but the people who lived in them made every effort to make them look like corrugated houses.

"Would you live in a trailer?" Kirsten asked as they stopped at the front directory. It reminded Linda of the buzzers at apartment buildings; this one had lot numbers with names next to them.

"I'd live anywhere with you," Linda replied, idling in front of the directory while she looked for the name Lindstrom.

"That's so sweet."

"Except a trailer park."

"Thanks. I'll remember that the next time you ask me to live in the woods."

Linda scanned halfway through the names, then found what she was looking for. Claire Lindstrom lived at #32, Delaware Drive. All the roads in the park were called drives. It added to the sense that residents were not just living in tin cans waiting to be sucked up by a tornado.

It took Linda just a few minutes to find Delaware Drive in the small maze of roads that all circled back to the entrance. Three homes down she found #32 and was surprised by how well-kept it was. There was a skirt around the bottom made of light blue shingles, a common technique of hiding the undercarriage: some of the homes were flush to the ground, while some rested on cinder blocks. Claire's was one of the latter. Linda imagined all the animals that could nest and find shelter under a trailer like this.

There were flowers along the front that managed to hang on despite the October weather, looking none the worse for the previous day's storm. The trailer itself was white with blue shutters on the windows in a shade darker than the skirt. It looked, overall, like a trailer that might house a young couple, possibly with a child and a dog.

"As you sure this is the right one?" Kirsten asked.

"We're going to find out," Linda said, parking in front of the trailer, careful not to put her wheels on the grass.

They got out of the car. Linda checked herself quickly, making sure she didn't look ruffled from all the time they'd spent driving. She wasn't sure what to expect, or even if Claire Lindstrom would be home. Or, for that matter, if she still lived here. According to Grace she had neglected to send a birthday card. It could be an oversight, or it could mean Claire had moved on to somewhere else or possibly to the afterlife.

The front door had three metal steps leading up to it. Linda led the way as she climbed the stairs and raised her hand to knock on the door.

The knock never happened. Just as Linda was about to politely rap her knuckles, the door swung open and a hunting rifle appeared, pointed directly at Linda's chest. Holding the rifle was a tiny woman with wrinkles for a face, bones for a body dressed loosely in skin, and eyes that could be those of a twelve-year-old, so sharp and clear and, for the moment, filled with suspicion.

Linda kept control of herself, showing neither alarm nor fear.

"Good afternoon," she said.

The woman did not speak. She kept the gun pointed up.

"We're looking for Claire Lindstrom," Kirsten said.

"Yeah, well," the woman said, "Claire Lindstrom was looking for you first."

It was a strange thing to say; it told Linda that someone had warned Lindstrom they were coming. She would worry later about how that could be.

"Are you Claire?" Linda asked.

"What do you think?" the woman said. "Now just go back down the steps, get in your car and head on out. I have nothing to say to you."

"How did you know we were coming?" asked Linda.

"Never mind that," said Claire. She pointed slightly with the rifle barrel, indicating their car. "You ought to just do as I say and drive back wherever you came from."

Thinking quickly, Linda said, "We just came from Marge's

Diner, actually. Grace Hinkley said you missed her last birthday."

Linda could see confusion cross Claire's face.

"How do you know Grace?"

"We met her at the diner. Never saw her before, never spoke to her before, but she asked us to tell you that. She's worried about you."

"Do I look like someone who needs worrying about?"

"No, Miss Lindstrom, you don't," said Linda. "You look like someone who can take care of herself, and I don't doubt you'd pull that trigger in an instant if you felt threatened. So you can keep it pointed on me if that helps. We're not here to cause you trouble."

Linda could see Claire relax. The gun shifted downward but she kept it securely in her hands.

"What are you here for, then?"

"We wanted to ask you about the Cliff's Edge."

"That son of a bitch is dead," said Claire. "That's all I know about the Cliff's Edge, and all I want to know. Not my life anymore, hasn't been for forty years."

"That's what I was hoping to talk to you about," Linda said. "Forty years ago. What happened. Why you left."

A long moment passed. Linda could tell Claire was making a decision, weighing whatever she'd been told against the reality of the two women in front of her.

"Come in, then," Claire said. "I'll give you ten minutes, but not on my stoop. Neighbors already think I'm crazy. Works to my favor, by the way. I don't like but two or three of them."

Claire let the rifle slide down to her side. She turned and walked back into her trailer, with Linda and Kirsten following cautiously behind.

The interior was as neat and tidy as the outside. A beige carpet gave the front room a lightness, and the furniture, while old, was not worn or sagged. There was a fake fireplace along one wall, with several knick-knacks on its mantle. A pastel checked couch faced the fireplace, with matching single recliners angled opposite it.

"Have a seat," Claire said, waving toward the recliners.

Linda and Kirsten each sat in one, while Claire eased herself onto the couch, laying the gun on a coffee table within reach.

Linda could tell they would not be offered coffee or tea, and that when Claire said they had ten minutes she meant it.

"Who told you we were coming?" Linda asked again.

"It doesn't matter," said Claire. "She was just looking out for me, that's all."

She. Linda wondered if it could be Lucille Proctor, or Betsy, or Grace for that matter. But Proctor wouldn't know where they were. And why would anyone call to warn her about them? Warn her of *what*? Maybe the rifle was the point. Maybe whoever had planted an idea in Claire Lindstrom's head had hoped her hand was unsteady at this age and that the gun would go off.

"You got nine minutes now," Claire said. "I don't talk about the past, so make it quick and don't expect much."

"Why did you leave?" asked Kirsten. "And why did everyone think you'd vanished?"

"Two questions, one answer: because I wanted it. Wanted to get out of Lonesome Pointe, and didn't want anyone to know where I was going."

"Grace knew," Linda said. "Is she the one who told you we were coming?"

"You keep asking that," said Claire. "It bugs me, so I'll just tell you. I've been friends with Dolores Drover for years. I kept an eye out for her when she was growing up. Not the sharpest tack in the box, so to speak. Girl needed someone other than her no-account father looking after her. He'd dead, she's got the motel, and justice prevailed, if you ask me."

The answers were creating more questions for Linda, but she knew she had to stay focused and worry about much of it later, like how Dolores Drover knew they were coming and why she would mislead Claire about their intentions—something she must have done to get them greeted with a gun barrel.

Kirsten leaned forward, her elbows on her knees. "What happened to make you want to leave?"

"You haven't spent much time in Lonesome Pointe, have you?" Claire said.

"It seems like a nice enough town," Kirsten replied.

"Wasn't such a nice town then."

"How's that?" Linda asked.

"I'd owned that place for ten years. The motel. Called it the Seaview then, thought I could make a go of it."

"Ten years is a good run," Kirsten said.

"You think so? Ten years of getting by. Ten years of cleaning motel rooms and finding a fifty cent tip on the nightstand? I couldn't afford much help, and what I got never stuck around long. It was hard work, Miss …"

"Kirsten McClellan, and this is Linda Sikorsky."

"I would've asked you that sooner but I didn't expect to see you in my home."

"And we should have introduced ourselves," Linda said. "My apologies. You were saying?"

"The Seaview was a silly dream I had," Claire continued. "Young people are known for those. But after a decade I was ready to get out, and the good people of the community were ready to have me gone. They didn't like having the Seaview outside their town. They didn't care for me, and I didn't care for them. So when the twins went missing right after I sold the place to Russell Drover, I figured it was as good a time as any to get the hell out. Didn't have a going away party, didn't tell anyone where I was going, except Grace and Dolores. Everybody else could go to hell."

"I thought you didn't like Russell Drover," Kirsten said.

"I didn't. That's why I sold the place to him!" Claire finally smiled, accompanying it with a quick laugh.

Linda had been listening carefully and caught something Kirsten seemed to have missed.

"You just said you left after the twins went missing," she said.

Claire Lindstrom's face darkened. "Did I?"

"Yes, you did," said Linda. "What twins were those?"

Linda was worried the conversation would now be seen by Claire as an interrogation. She did not want that, knowing it could end their ten minutes early. She had also never stopped glancing at the rifle.

Linda could see Claire thinking it over. She would either keep talking, or they would be told to leave.

"The Bradley boys," she said at last. "Todd and Christopher. I'll never forget their names, and I'll never forget their faces. Sweetest boys you could meet. And somebody in that town had a sweet tooth, if you catch my drift."

"What happened to them?" Kirsten asked.

"Nobody knows," said Claire. "Nobody knew then, either, but they guessed plenty. Some people even thought it was me, if that isn't the stupidest thing you ever heard."

The information was swirling around in Linda's mind. Suddenly this was not just about Cayley Drees anymore. Or maybe it was. Was it possible the young reporter had discovered something about the twins' disappearance? Where did this past intersect with the present, and had it cost Cayley her life?

"Is the family still around?" Linda asked. "The Bradleys, I mean."

"Long gone," Claire said. "Mother killed herself about a year after the twins were taken. Have to say it that way, too. Somebody took them. Then the father, Dickey is all I knew him by, he moved away. No idea where to. He might be dead by now, too, or drunk forty years in a bar somewhere."

None of it made sense to Linda at the moment. Could Russell Drover have been the one who took the boys? Dolores would have been a child then. She didn't know how old Meredith Vesey was, but she had no reason to think she would have been more than a teenager herself.

"Do you know Meredith Vesey?" she asked.

"I know of her," Claire said. "That's enough. Last of her line. The Veseys were some of my loudest critics back then. They hated the motel. But they didn't have anything to do with the twins disappearing, I'm sure of it, and Meredith wasn't but fourteen or fifteen then."

Maybe she knew something, Linda thought. Maybe Dolores knew something, too. Children are far more observant than many people wanted to admit. They see, they hear, and they can be counted on not to speak, if given the right incentive.

"Your time's up," Claire said. She wasn't hard about it, and Linda sensed the conversation was one Claire Lindstrom would rather not have had. She seemed deflated, as if her avoidance of the past had failed her for the few minutes they'd been in her home.

"Thank you very much for talking to us," Linda said, raising herself from the chair.

"Just don't say it's been a pleasure," said Claire, "because it hasn't. Don't know what you learned, or why you wanted to know it, but you're not dangerous. You'd be dead on my front steps if you were."

"I'm sure of that," Linda said, smiling, and something passed between them. One strong woman showing courtesy to another, both unafraid to pull a trigger if they had to.

Claire stood from the couch and walked them to the door, leaving the rifle on the coffee table. As they were exiting the trailer, she said, "You see Grace again, tell her I mailed the damn card. Sometimes these things get lost at the post office, it happens."

"If we see her we'll tell her," Linda said.

"But you won't. No problem, I'll send her another one."

They left the old woman standing in her doorway. She lingered there, almost as if she wished she'd given them twenty minutes instead of ten.

They got into the car and Linda started the ignition.

"It's all connected," Kirsten said, sliding her seatbelt across her shoulder.

"Yes it is," Linda replied. "Somewhere between those children's abduction and the death of Cayley Drees, it all comes together."

"You think Russell Drover took those boys?"

"I don't know, Sweetie. But I think Meredith Vesey, whoever she is, has an idea."

"She was a kid then."

"Kids know things," Linda said, putting the car into drive and pulling away.

She had only been eight years old when her father bled to death outside a grocery store he'd gone to because Linda had run out of her favorite cereal. Kids knew things, they certainly did, like how brutal life can be, and how quickly everything can change.

"Where to now?" Kirsten asked.

"Back to the All Pointes. I want to ask someone about these twins, someone whose business it is to know what happened and when."

"Lucille Proctor."

"None other."

Linda looked at the dashboard clock. It was now past two o'clock. The afternoon was passing and she did not want to have to call Serenity House again.

They drove out of Big View Mobile Estates and back toward the highway, unaware of the car parked on another drive, in front of another trailer, with Lenny Winfrow low in the seat as he called his boss. Meredith Vesey would not be happy with the news, not happy at all.

21

THE CLIFF'S EDGE

IT TOOK Lenny less than an hour to get back to the Cliff's Edge. He'd broken the speed limit by double digits, trusting his luck not to get stopped along the way. The Drees murder was about as big an event as Lonesome Pointe ever saw and he counted on the sheriff and his deputies being preoccupied for a while.

He had no idea where the women were going once they left the trailer park. He'd wanted to follow them, but Meredith had told him to go back to the hotel immediately. Sheriff McBride had been there putting his nose where it could get cut off, and she needed Lenny there in case he made a return visit, possibly with a warrant. Meredith thought it wisest to have the front desk clerk where he was supposed to be.

"What about the bitches?" he'd said, watching Linda's car pull away as he turned off the road.

"Leave them be. McBride's my concern right now. Dolores was there when he showed up, thank God."

Lenny had snorted at that and hoped she hadn't heard. *You don't believe in God*, he'd thought. *Or you just think you're Him.*

"Whatever you say, Boss," he'd said, making a quick U-turn and depressing the accelerator as much as he dared.

Forty-five minutes later he was back behind the desk, wondering what the point of it was. They had no guests scheduled to check in and the ones who were still there planned on staying. Anybody who hadn't high-tailed it by now would be charged another day, except the two women. He knew he'd see them again when they came back to drop off the key, and he'd be glad to be done with them. The storm had dropped something unexpected and unwanted at the Cliff's Edge. The sooner they blew over like the clouds, the better.

He was counting out cash in the register drawer, kept in case someone needed change for smokes or rubbers, or one of the candy bars he had displayed on the counter. He ate most of them himself and had to replace them every other day. He'd just finished with the one dollar bills when a man came in, startling him. He jumped, a bad sign for Lenny. Nobody came up on him like that. It meant he was more on edge than he admitted to himself. The dykes, the sheriff, the dead reporter. He didn't like what it was all adding up to.

"Can I help you?" Lenny said, shoving the bills into the register. "You need a room? We got plenty."

Trevor Wilcox did not smile at the man. He was Trevor again, having left Daniel Wiley back in Ogunquit. Considering his mission, it was only right. Just as he had stopped being Trevor when he left Lonesome Pointe twenty years ago, he had stopped being Daniel when he decided to put an end to his running once and for all.

"I was hoping to speak to the owner," Trevor said.

He had his hands in his jacket pockets, and Lenny suddenly wondered what he might have in one of them. A pistol? A recorder? Something was not right about this man. Lenny slid off his stool and stood, wanting to be prepared. You can fall off a stool; it's much harder to fall off your feet.

"She's not here," Lenny said. "May not be back for a few days. Can I help you with something?"

Lenny could tell by the man's reaction he was surprised to hear the owner was a "she."

"So Dolores came back?" Trevor said.

Back? Lenny was even more suspicious now. He did not recognize this man, but *back* indicated he'd been here before, at some point. *Back* meant he knew things, at least something of the history of the Cliff's Edge and the Drovers.

"I didn't catch your name," said Lenny. "I'm Lenny Winfrow, I manage the place."

It was a lie, but who cared? He'd told lots of people he was the manager. Dolores wouldn't like him saying that, but the Cliff's Edge was not the kind of place people stuck around to chat with the new owner about what her desk clerk said or didn't say.

"My name is Trevor Wilcox. I used to live here. Well, not *here*, but in Lonesome Pointe. I knew Russell Drover. I knew his daughter too, before she moved away. And Meredith Vesey, of course."

"Of course."

"I'm guessing Meredith still lives in town."

It had the sound of a statement, not a question. Lenny's silent alarm system, the one in his reptile brain, was blaring now. Predators such as himself depended on hunches, and his told him the man standing in front of him was here for no good.

"Never met the woman myself," Lenny lied. "But she's still here. Got that big house on the hill."

The man seemed to be thinking, standing quietly and glancing at his shoes. Finally, he looked up at Lenny and said, "Thank you, you've been most helpful, Mr. Winfrow."

Lenny knew he hadn't been helpful at all and he wanted something more from this stranger.

"You want me to give Dolores a message?" he said.

"No," Trevor said. "No thank you."

You're too damn calm, Lenny thought. "What did you say your name was?"

"Trevor Wilcox. We were just kids."

Lenny stared at him: what the hell was that supposed to mean, "just kids"? Just kids *when what?*

"I can let you have a room half price today," Lenny said. "Storm's over, everybody's moved on."

Trevor smiled and it sent a shiver through Lenny. *Too damn calm*, he thought again. *Killer calm. I know that one myself.*

The man nodded and turned around, about to leave.

"Where you going?" Lenny asked to his back.

Trevor waited a moment, then said, "To a house on a hill."

He walked out, letting the door shut behind him.

Lenny grabbed his phone and dialed, watching as the man got into his car.

"What now?" Meredith said when she answered.

Lenny could tell her patience had worn thin, probably along with her nerves.

"You got company coming," he said.

He began to tell her about the strange visitor who was headed her way.

22

THE ALL POINTES BULLETIN

LINDA DROVE faster than she should have. She never counted on her position as a retired cop to get her off in the event of a traffic stop. She was also law-abiding by nature and had only been pulled over twice in the past ten years driving her own vehicle. Each time she was given a nod and a warning she knew was more lenient than most people got, and each time she felt guilty, knowing she'd been extended a privilege not afforded to others. But the day was passing, and things were slowly coming together. She had no idea where the various threads would meet, or how tightly they would prove to be knotted, but she saw their convergence, there in the distance, and she was gaining on it.

They made it back to the All Pointes Bulletin in just over thirty minutes. Kirsten had not nagged Linda about breaking the speed limit. She was, overall, an annoying passenger-seat driver (Linda knew the term "backseat driver" came from an earlier time, but it made little sense; most harping aimed at a driver came from someone sitting next to them). This relief from the usual criticism could only be because Kirsten wanted out of Lonesome Pointe as much as Linda wanted to know what happened in room #6. The sooner they found answers, the sooner they could leave.

"What do you think we're going to learn here?" Kirsten asked as Linda parked the car in the same spot they'd taken earlier.

"History, I hope," Linda said. "This is all part of the one larger picture and I'm trying to get it into focus. The Cliff's Edge, Russell Drover's suicide—if it was a suicide—and now these twins disappearing. It's all connected."

"You're making assumptions, Linda. Is that a good thing for any detective, retired or otherwise?"

"You mean, would Rox Harmony make assumptions," Linda replied. "And the answer is yes, yes she would. People in police work make assumptions all the time. We have to. We can't act on them until those assumptions have been proven correct by evidence, but we certainly make them. Hell, Sweetie, half the job is chasing your assumptions, the things that seem most likely to you. But a good cop, a good detective, is willing to be wrong."

"Is that what you're hoping?" Kirsten said as they got out of the car.

"I can't say yet, because I don't know what I'm wrong about. The only thing I know is that a woman at the beginning of her life was murdered and left in a field. That's a fact. But why? There could be many reasons, or none we'll ever know."

Rudy was back at his station when they entered the office, typing on his computer. He looked up at them with surprise; he had not expected to see them again.

"Well, hello, ladies. Did you forget something?"

"No," Linda said. "But I had a few questions I'd like to ask Ms. Proctor if she's available."

"Let me check," Rudy said, picking up his phone and dialing his boss's extension.

Linda turned away, not wanting Rudy to think she was listening to him, or, worse, trying to read his computer screen. Whatever he was looking at was none of her business, nor did she care, but people did not like the feeling of being watched.

"She said to come into her office," Rudy announced. "You know the way."

Linda thought there was something not quite right about Rudy's reaction to them. Had he been merely surprised to see them, or was there a hint of displeasure? And why would he be bothered by their return? She told herself it was ridiculous to think this, that her imagination was getting the best of her; then she led Kirsten past the front desk, down the hall and into Lucille Proctor's office.

Lucille looked tired. It had been a long day and it was only mid-afternoon. Linda doubted the normal stresses of the job would take such a toll—Proctor had been doing this for many years and must be used to the demands—but one of her young reporters, who may also have been a friend for all Linda knew, was now dead less than twelve hours. It was a big story, probably the biggest Webley County had seen in many years, and it was the responsibility of the All Pointes and its editor to cover it.

"What can I help you with, Ms. Sikorsky?" Lucille said.

Linda and Kirsten took the same seats at the small table they'd had earlier. Lucille remained at her desk this time, talking across it to them. She didn't seem perturbed as much as weary: she had not bothered to close the door or stand to greet them.

"We just spoke to Claire Lindstrom," Linda said. She waited a moment for Lucille's response, then realized the name meant nothing to her. "The original owner of the Cliff's Edge."

"Oh, right," Lucille said, remembering the story the paper had run. "Did she tell you the place wasn't haunted? We kind of knew that."

"Actually, she told us about the disappearance forty years ago of two young boys, twins."

This time there was immediate recognition in Lucille's eyes. "I remember that," she said. "I was about twenty then. I was away at school but it was big news. The biggest since ..."

Since the murder of Cayley Drees, Linda thought.

"Anyway, how is this germane to the death of my reporter?"

"That's what we're trying to find out," Linda said. "What do you remember about it?"

Lucille sat back, letting her tense posture relax slightly. She put her hands on the arms of her chair and thought back to a time forty years ago when two young children vanished in broad daylight.

"All I remember," she said, "is that two very young boys—what were they, six or seven, something like that?—were in town with their mother. She turned her back for a minute, which always seems to be the case, it doesn't take more than that to lure a child away, and the next thing everyone knew these boys were gone forever."

"They were never found?" Kirsten asked.

"Neither dead nor alive," said Lucille. "It tore the family apart. There was a divorce, if I'm remembering that correctly, and the mother killed herself."

"Were there siblings? What happened to the father?"

"I'd have to think about that. I was only twenty then, remember, and not living here at the time. As tragic and horrible as that kidnapping was, life goes on, as we say too often. Just like it will go on now that Cayley's dead. I won't be forgetting this one so easily."

Linda could see Lucille's eyes water; she doubted this kind of show of emotion happened often, and did not want to add to the woman's grief by staying too long.

"Do you think there's a connection?" Lucille asked. "Between the two events, I mean."

"Yes, yes I do," Linda said. "I don't know how they're

connected or in what manner, but the crossing point of it all is the Cliff's Edge. Maybe the boys were taken there. Or maybe whoever took them stayed there."

"How do you propose to find this information out?"

"I'm not sure," Linda said, and she wasn't. It was a baffling case, with tentacles stretching outward in several directions from that rundown motel by the side of the road.

"You asked me a minute ago about siblings," Lucille said. "I'm remembering this now, at least I think I am. The father left town, the mother was found in her bathtub with her veins opened. But there was an older sister, Rebecca. She stayed."

"Was she placed with relatives?" said Kirsten.

"There weren't any as I recall. It's unusual but it happens. And sometimes the relatives just don't want to raise a child, or at least not another one. She ended up living with the pastor and his wife ... yes, that's what happened. They're both deceased now, too. Bayliss, I think that was their name. Becky was taken in by them and still lives in Lonesome Pointe. But you may not get much information from her."

"Why's that?" said Linda.

"She's ... developmentally challenged. I'm not sure what language we're supposed to use now with these things. Differently abled? *Developmentally* differently abled? Not much, more like mild autism. High functioning for sure, you wouldn't know she had problems unless you were told, which I just did. She lives on her own, and works at the Good Friends thrift store. She's been there longer than I've been at the All Pointes. Most people don't even know she's the sister of those boys. I'd all but forgotten myself. Life goes on, as I said."

Linda was weighing her options. She was very hesitant to question a woman who would now be at least fifty, and one whose mental acuity might not be up to remembering old, painful details.

"What about Meredith Vesey?" Linda asked.

She saw visible distaste on Lucille's face. "What about her?"

"We're told Dolores Drover, Russell's daughter, spends time with Meredith. I keep thinking it's possible they saw or heard something when they were children."

"Like what happened to the Bradley twins," Lucille said. "Why wouldn't they have said something then, or any time since?"

"I don't know why," Linda said. "But I want to find out. I also think whoever contacted Cayley, her anonymous source, knows what happened, too."

"And that's what got her killed," said Lucille. She leaned forward, lowering her voice. "Do you think Russell Drover took those boys?"

"I think anything is possible," Linda said. "I can understand why Dolores, who couldn't have been much older than the twins herself, would not turn her father in. Kids don't often do that, at least not forty years ago. But she may have known what happened. I don't know where Vesey fits in, or the caller who got Cayley involved. But some kind of answer is bubbling to the surface and I'm going to raise the heat, just enough to see what's at the bottom."

Linda stood up, followed by Kirsten. It was time to leave Lucille Proctor to her job and her sorrow. This time Lucille stood, meeting them at her office door.

Lowering her voice still further, Lucille said, "Do you carry a firearm by any chance, Ms. Sikorsky?"

A moment of truth: to say no was to lie by omission (she did not technically carry her gun) and lying was something Linda and Kirsten did not do to each other. To say yes was to invite a conversation from her weapon-averse wife, probably before sundown, about why she had brought her gun.

"I do," Linda said. "But not on my person. It's in a locked case in our car trunk."

"What?" said Kirsten, surprised.

"We'll talk about it later," Linda said. "I'm sorry, Honey, I just don't take chances. Two women alone on the road, it's not my nature to travel unprotected."

"I have to agree with you," Lucille said. "I don't own a gun myself, but I carry pepper spray and a very efficient Swiss Army knife."

"Why do you ask if I carry a firearm?"

"I just think you're going places with this where you might need one," said Lucille. She then let them out of her office, watching as they headed down the hallway.

Linda wondered if they would ever see Lucille Proctor again. She hoped so, or at least a phone call, to tell her what they'd found at the end of this road. She'd promised Lucile that much. Proctor had a newspaper to run, as she'd told them, and this was all shaping up to be front page news. She liked the woman, too, and thought they might make good friends someday. It was unlikely to happen, but friendships had come into her life through even more unexpected encounters.

Life goes on.

They walked passed Rudy at his desk. He nodded a goodbye, saying nothing, and Linda again had the feeling there was something not quite right about the young man. He seemed nervous to see them and she could not think of any reason he would be.

Back in the car, Kirsten asked, "Where to now? Don't think I'm unaware of the time, and don't think we won't talk about your gun. What if somebody breaks into the trunk?"

"They can't get into the case, it's expensive, sturdy and secured with a combination. As for where we're going, I'd like to visit a thrift store in town."

"Are you sure that's a good idea?"

"Am I sure any idea is good at this point? I don't know, but I see something in the distance, an answer, and I have to go there, Babe. I can't help myself. Cayley deserves it. Those twins deserve it."

Do I deserve it? Linda imagined Kirsten asking, but she did not. Instead she said, "Fine. You're driving, you take us where you want to go, but you've just added another night at Serenity House, and this one's on you."

"Deal," said Linda, starting the car and pulling away from the All Pointes.

23

FOR OLD TIMES' SAKE

THE LAST time Trevor Wilcox saw Meredith Vesey's house he was twelve years old. Between then and when he left Lonesome Point he'd seen it only from a distance, simply because of the house's elevation. But while he'd viewed it from far off with dread all those intervening years, he had never again stood in its driveway, looked at its imposing porch, or knocked on its front door, as he was doing now. He had not needed directions today; when you see a house on a hill, you know where it is. What he needed, he told himself as he waited for someone to answer, were several stiff drinks.

He knew the past could not be outrun, he had tried. He knew those things we attempt to escape are prepared to wait a lifetime to catch up to us, as they had for him. He also knew, after seeing the news reports of Cayley Drees's murder, that the past was now the present and his part in events would have to become known. He had carried their secrets his entire life. He had wanted to tell someone, and by doing so he had gotten her killed. He did not doubt there was a connection, even though the police and townspeople were surely talking of predators on dark roads and what women needed to do to protect themselves. They would want to think it was random. Random tragedy makes more sense and is more easily tolerated than thinking a killer lived among them. Trevor knew better, and he believed Meredith knew better, too. He did not know what her involvement might be, but he was sure she was part of it somehow. The time had come to confront her, to tell her the past had come to collect its due and he'd had no choice but to welcome it, the way one welcomes an undertaker to the house.

The door opened, startling Trevor who'd been lost in his thoughts. He didn't know what he was expecting—a butler or servant of some kind?—but the person who smiled at him from just inside the foyer was Dolores Drover. He remembered her. They'd left town about the same time, but for very different reasons. She looked so much the way she had the last time he'd seen her, only now she was two decades older, heavier, showing the signs of age and gravity.

"Can I help you?" she said. She clearly did not recognize him.

"I'm Trevor Wilcox."

"Is that name supposed to mean something to me?"

"I lived here. Well ... not here, but in Lonesome Pointe. I used to play at your father's motel sometimes."

Her eyes widened as she remembered the boy who used to hang around the Cliff's Edge, always with Meredith. He had not come back after that terrible tragedy with the twins, something she barely recalled. She had been only eleven when that happened, but eleven was old enough to have clear memories and she remembered Trevor. A shy boy, a follower.

"Can I help you with something?" she said.

The answer came from behind her as Meredith walked to the door, saying too loudly, "Trevor? Trevor Wilcox?"

Trevor stepped back slightly, as if threatened.

Meredith ignored his body language, gently pushing past Dolores and out onto her porch where she threw her arms around Trevor and pulled him close in an embrace.

"Oh my God," Meredith said. "I can't even guess how long it's been. Please, come in."

This was not at all what Trevor had expected and his mind was racing. Did she not remember the secrets they shared? Had she managed to bury the past while he had been going back to its grave year after year waiting for it to rise and apprehend him?

"Trevor?" she said, studying his face. "Are you all right?"

"I'm fine, Meredith, I just ... wasn't anticipating ..."

Meredith turned to Dolores. "You were probably too young to remember, but Trevor and I were best friends back in the day. *Way* back in the day."

"I think I do remember," Dolores said, and of course she did: her crush on Meredith Vesey started then. Even eleven-year-olds can have romantic fantasies, although they don't define them as such. Dolores only knew she was very attracted to the girl Meredith and she liked it so much when she came around the motel, mostly to play in the trees behind it or hang out with Meredith's older cousin Jeannine who did their housekeeping then. She had not paid any attention to the boy, who was now standing in front of her. They would have been close to the same age. She'd had no interest in boys and this one had been especially forgettable.

"Now get in this house, Trevor Wilcox!" Meredith said. She took him by the hand and led him inside, letting Dolores close the door behind them.

Trevor had little time to look at the foyer and the hallway Meredith pulled him down. It had been so many years since he'd been here that he could not remember if the paintings on the walls were the same, or if the crescent phone stand had been there; it probably had been, since so many people didn't have landlines anymore, and they certainly did not keep avocado Princess phones on stands in the entryway.

Meredith tugged him into a large living room, and this he remembered. He'd been here many times before the age of twelve. He'd played with Meredith in this room, cards mostly, but sometimes board games and always with just the two of them. If Meredith had other friends then, Trevor did not know of their existence. She'd needed only one true disciple, and here he was again.

Meredith pointed Trevor to one of two facing couches that looked to be as old as the telephone but in very well-kept condition. Trevor sat in one, Meredith took the other.

Dolores was about to sit down when Meredith said, "Did you pick up that dry cleaning yet like I asked you to, Dolores? It's been ready two days now."

"Oh, shoot," Dolores said. "I haven't had a chance. Can it wait awhile longer? I'd love to get caught up ..."

"With a man you don't remember?" Meredith said. "Not much to get caught up on, Sweetie." She knew calling Dolores "Sweetie" in front of someone would soften Dolores up. It was a public acknowledgement of their relationship and Dolores's importance to her.

"Well, if you insist. Can I bring you folks back something? An afternoon snack, maybe?"

"Nothing for me," said Trevor.

"That's a great idea," Meredith said, ignoring him. She knew an added stop would keep Dolores out for a while longer. "Maybe some cupcakes from Dotty's. We love Dotty's cupcakes, don't we, Dear?"

Dolores was beaming. She had been called "Sweetie" and "Dear" in less than a minute. And with a stranger present!

"Marble with vanilla frosting, you're favorite," Dolores said. "I'll be back in an hour."

"Take your time," Meredith said.

She waited for Dolores to leave the house. Once she heard the door close, she turned back to Trevor and said, "She's a lifesaver, really, doing errands for me to the dry cleaner, the grocery, the bank of course. I don't do online banking. I just don't trust the internet, do you?"

"I don't spend much time there," Trevor said.

"No, you don't." The words were flat, a statement rather than a question. "I thought you might be dead, Trevor. I looked, but you'd just vanished. That's not easy to do these days. But I get it. I keep a very low profile online myself. Who really has time for Facebook and all that social media madness? If I wanted to live in the modern age, I wouldn't be living here! Such a big house for just me and my parents. You remember my parents?"

"Your mother was always nice to me," he said.

"Why are you here?"

The turn in conversation was abrupt and threw Trevor off balance.

He took a moment to compose himself, then said, "You saw the news about that young reporter?"

"The one they found by the road this morning. Yes, I'm sorry to say. I saw it and I've been upset by it all day. I have to hide these things from Dolores, she's easily distressed."

"Was she distressed when her father was killed?"

"Excuse me?"

"Russell Drover did not commit suicide, Meredith. I knew that when I read the obituary."

"Then you read a different obituary from the one I saw, because it didn't mention a cause of death."

"It didn't have to," Trevor said. "I made some anonymous phone calls and discovered what I already knew: he'd ended his own life. At least that's what someone wanted people to think."

Meredith smiled at him, sending a shiver through his entire body.

"Is that when you called the reporter?" she said.

He heard a door open behind them. He remembered there being an exit in the kitchen that led out to the side yard. He'd played with Meredith there, too, sometimes hide and seek, sometimes darker games. He assumed Dolores had forgotten something and returned through the back door.

"Yes, that's when I called her," he said. "It's time, Meredith. Time to tell people what we know, time to bring it to an end."

"Actually," said Meredith, "I think it's time you met Lenny. Oh, wait, you already did."

Trevor turned, expecting to see Lenny Winfrow in the doorway, but somehow the man had come up behind him, standing over Trevor. Who is that quiet but someone skilled in the art of surprise? Trevor jerked around to see Lenny smiling down at him.

"I'd introduce you," Meredith said, "but there's no need for that. Lenny, this is Trevor, a very old friend from my childhood. Trevor, this is Lenny. He'll be your executioner today."

Trevor tried to jump, to get off the couch, but Lenny was too quick. In less than two seconds he had a chain around Trevor's neck, the kind people use to hang wallets and keys from their belts. A *choker chain*, aptly named.

Lenny yanked Trevor backward, pulling the chain as tightly as he could, embedding it deep into the flesh of Trevor's neck.

"Off the couch!" Meredith shouted. "I don't want him pissing himself on my furniture."

Lenny obliged, leaping over the couch with his hand still gripped to the chain. Trevor's face was bloated and purple. Lenny dragged him from the couch onto the floor, where he straddled him and kept strangling.

Sure enough, Trevor's bladder gave way and a dark, wet stain began to spread along the front of his pants.

Trevor flailed a last time, his arm brushing the coffee table that sat between the couches.

"My table!" Meredith shrieked, pulling it away before Trevor's seizing could do any damage. "My mother loved that table."

Meredith glanced at the grandfather clock. It had only been ten minutes since Dolores left but she did not want to take any chances.

"Please get him out of here," she said. "Just make sure he's dead."

"Where you want me to take him, Boss?" Lenny said. He was still on top of Trevor, hoping his own erection would go down. He didn't want Meredith seeing that murder made him hard. She'd think he was one of *them*. He didn't mind admitting to bisexuality, but he wasn't queer. It was the killing that got him stiff, not the killed.

"I don't care," Meredith said. "He was his own worst enemy. He wanted Trevor Wilcox gone, and he succeeded. You can't miss somebody no one's heard of in twenty years."

Lenny got up, confident his cock had flattened enough not to be noticeable. He was winded. Killing was exciting but it required exertion. He took Trevor by the heels and began dragging him toward the back door, careful not to pull his shoes off.

"Maybe take him out to the old Garland farm, that barn's all but fallen in on itself. Nobody goes there."

"Good a place as any," Lenny said. "We can always move him later."

Meredith slid the table back in place and crossed to the couch, fluffing the pillows where Trevor had sat. She would tell Dolores something came up for their visitor, some kind of family emergency and he'd left in a hurry.

"Before you go," Meredith said.

"Yes, Boss?"

"Pull his car into the garage. We can't very well have a dead man's car in the driveway. And don't say anything to Dolores. She doesn't know about this."

"Yes, Boss."

She glanced at the clock again, compulsively checking the time. Only five minutes had passed, but she wanted things cleaned up long before Dolores came home. The idiot knew about the reporter, and she knew about her own father because she'd taken so much pleasure in the deed. But some things she did not know. Some things only Meredith Vesey and Trevor Wilcox knew, and now she held those secrets alone. She intended for it to stay that way.

The garage did not have windows and was not used for their cars; instead it had been used for storage ever since Meredith was a child. Her father had kept a small wood shop there, and her mother had stored a lifetime's detritus. Meredith had cleaned much of it out after her father's death and there was enough room for Trevor's car. Meredith watched from the front window as Lenny parked a dead man's car in the garage. He closed the door and a moment later drove off in his own car with Trevor's body in the trunk. Once he was safely gone, Meredith locked the garage and hid the key. Dolores, needy and pliable, would not question why the door was locked. She'd not shown any curiosity about it yet and there was no reason to now.

She finished tidying up the room, making it look as if their visitor had stayed but a moment. They would be alone again, just Meredith, her sweet Dolores, and the memories never spoken of between these walls.

24

GOOD FRIENDS

GOOD FRIENDS Thrift store reminded Linda of many she'd been in over the years, especially with her mother. Estelle Sikorsky still enjoyed browsing the dress and sweater racks at the Goodwill and some of the lesser known local operations set up to fund one charity or another. The family budget had been tight after they'd moved to Philadelphia, requiring Estelle to shop as smartly as possible. Young Linda had been accustomed to wearing clothes another child had worn before her. It never bothered her, and Estelle was gifted at finding the best items, knowing when the new donations were put out each week. Linda even thought it had something to do with her own fondness for stores that sold vintage items, and why she had started one herself. There was a big difference between a Goodwill and *For Pete's Sake*, but there was also some essential commonality.

"Maybe I can stay here and shop while you catch a killer," Kirsten said. "Pick me up on your way out of town and we'll be in Cape Haven for an early dinner."

"I'm trying," Linda said. She knew Kirsten's patience had grown thin. They should be sitting on a porch at Serenity House by now dipping biscotti into cappuccinos.

There were only four or five people in the store, and two of them worked there. Linda could tell by the blue smocks they wore, complete with name tags.

"Can I help you find something?" an elderly gentleman said, walking up to them. His name tag identified him as Fred. He had a box of barrettes in his hand with a sign on the side that said, "25 Cents Ea." "We just got some new pantsuits in, if you like that kind of thing."

Linda got the feeling he did not like pantsuits on a woman.

"I was hoping to speak to Rebecca," Linda said.

"That would be Becky at the cash register," he replied. "Are you friends of hers?"

"Not exactly," said Kirsten. "We just wanted to have a chat."

"About what?"

Linda didn't care for the man's curiosity; then she wondered if he was just being protective. Rebecca Bradley had, by Lucille's account, remained in a town in which her brothers had been abducted and her mother had committed suicide. Her father had left Lonesome Pointe and not taken her with him, leaving her to be raised by a preacher and his wife. Someone needed to protect the girl who was now a woman on the other side of middle age.

"I wanted to ask her about her brothers," Linda said. She'd decided honesty would be the best approach. The old guy might have a nice smile but his eyes said he was nobody's fool.

"She doesn't know anything," said the man with Fred on his name tag.

"I really would appreciate hearing that from her."

"And who would you be?"

"We're visiting," said Linda. "We stayed at the Cliff's Edge last night and we saw the news about that young reporter being killed."

Linda leaned toward him, lowering her voice. Offering what sounded like privileged information often worked to get people talking, if only for the pleasure of gossip.

"I think there is some connection between what happened to the Bradley twins and what happened to the reporter."

"Really?" said Fred, a look of astonishment on his face. "Well, then, you're welcome to talk to Becky. But these are things—the whole sad affair—she doesn't talk about. It's been a very long time, Miss ..."

"Sikorsky, Linda Sikorsky. And this is Kirsten McClellan."

"Pleased to meet you," said Kirsten.

"If you really think it will help," Fred said. "That sort of thing just doesn't happen here."

Linda wondered if he meant the twins being abducted or Cayley Drees being killed, possibly both.

He waved toward Rebecca, who was alone at the register. "Becky! Becky, these two women would like to talk to you a minute. Come on over, I'll take the register."

Becky looked around uncertainly, as if a rush of customers might come through the door and she would be needed at the cash register.

"It's okay," Fred said, walking toward her. He said something to her Linda could not hear, and a moment later Becky came walking up to them.

She was a pretty woman, Linda noticed. She did not appear frail or frightened, only unsure of why strangers would want to talk to her. She was a good foot shorter than Linda, and thin. She wore her hair in a ponytail that was mostly gray with some strands of brown in it.

"Can I help you?" Becky asked.

Noticing her shyness, Linda thought it might be best if they did not double-team her. She glanced at Kirsten, who immediately understood: she smiled and headed off to a rack of blouses, pretending to slowly look through them.

"My name is Linda Sikorsky, and I used to be a police officer."

Becky looked startled.

"I'm not here for anything you've done, Rebecca."

"Why, then?"

"I'm here because I understand … your brothers disappeared a long time ago."

Becky cocked her head at this, as if trying to make sense of it.

"It's been forty years," she said. "I don't have anything else to say. Nobody's asked me about that since I was a girl."

Maybe they should have, Linda thought, but said, "I imagine a lot of people from back then aren't around anymore." *Like your father, your mother, and the pastor who raised you.*

"They're all gone," said Rebecca, "I'm the only one still alive. The Sheriff from those days passed on, too. Why would you want to know about something hardly anyone remembers?"

Linda sensed that whatever developmental challenges Rebecca Bradley had were not pronounced. She seemed like any other fifty-year-old woman living in a small town.

"I'm just curious," Linda said. "I know the case was never solved and I thought maybe it was time to take another look at it."

"Did Sheriff McBride send you?"

"In a roundabout way, but not directly, no. I was told about your brothers by the woman who used to own the old motel."

"The Cliff's Edge," Rebecca said, and her face darkened. "I don't go there. Nobody good goes there."

Linda wondered what she meant by that. Then she remembered Sheriff McBride telling her the children had been warned away from playing there. A boogeyman was a handy tool in some parents' toolboxes.

"Did your brothers go there?" Linda asked carefully.

"They were too young," Becky said. "They couldn't drive there, now could they? And Mama always told us not to walk on the road, it was too dangerous. You could ride a bike there, but it was risky. Every couple years somebody got hit by a car, thrown in a ditch."

"Were you with your brothers the day … when they went missing?"

"I already told the police this, a dozen times. I was at home. Mama took Todd and Christopher shopping with her. She let them play outside the general store —it's gone now, most of the town looked different back then. There was a big wooden Indian out front and a pony you could put quarters in and ride for a couple minutes. They were riding that pony, last time Mama saw them. She wasn't a bad person."

Linda had a sudden flash of guilt. She was taking this woman back to a place she did not want to go, reminding her of family lost, a mother so wracked with grief and regret that she ended her own life.

"There were never any suspects?" she asked.

"Oh, there were lots of them," Becky said. "Every man passing through town, and a woman or two. We're not far from the highway, it wouldn't take much to grab the boys and be in another state by supper."

"What about Russell Drover, the man who took over the Cliff's Edge about that time?"

"People thought things, sure. Nobody liked him. But just because you don't like someone doesn't mean they steal children."

"No, it doesn't," Linda said. *It doesn't mean they* don't *steal children, either*, she thought.

"I need to get back to work," Becky said, anxiously looking at the register where Fred was fidgeting with boxes of buttons and ribbons.

"Did Todd and Christopher ever go off with other people?" Linda asked. "You know, people they trusted, like a school teacher or a sheriff's deputy?"

"No. Mama taught us over and over, don't talk to strangers. If they offer you anything, scream and run."

Linda knew that kidnappers sometimes worked with children of their own. It was rare, but it happened, especially if the intention was to take the boys and keep them imprisoned, or raise them with new identities. *Might they still be alive?* she wondered. The thought both excited and horrified her.

"What about other kids?" she said. "Would they go off with another child?"

"I suppose so," Becky said. "But that doesn't make any sense, does it? Listen, it's been nice talking but Fred needs help. He looks nervous, I can tell. He needs me."

"Becky, thank you so much for speaking to me," Linda said. She waved at Kirsten, who came walking slowly back.

"I wish I could help," Becky said. "It was a long time ago."

"I understand," Linda said.

They walked with Becky back to the cash register. Linda thanked Fred and Becky again, then led Kirsten out to the car.

Her thoughts were jumbled but trying to coalesce. If the twins would not go with an adult, even one they knew, who would they go with? Would they leave with another child they didn't know? What about a child they *did* know?

"I have a feeling we'll be getting to Cape Haven late," Kirsten said. There wasn't so much anger in her tone as resignation.

"I'll make it up to you," Linda said. "And I'll try to get us there for dinner, I really will. But I want to talk to someone, it's time."

"And who would that someone be?" Kirsten asked, snapping her seatbelt shut.

"That someone would be Meredith Vesey."

"Do you know where she lives?"

Linda leaned forward and pointed to a hill in the distance. "You see that house up there?"

Kirsten peered through the windshield. "You can't miss it," she said.

"That's where we're going."

She put the car in gear and drove out of the lot, sensing things were coming together and dreading what she would find there.

"Do you carry a firearm by any chance, Ms. Sikorsky?"

Lucille Proctor's question came back to her, sounding even more like a warning than it had when she'd asked.

Why yes, Lucille, I do.

She wondered if the time had come to take the gun out of its case in the trunk. She hoped not, but she knew that decision would be determined by events. It could go one way, or it could go another. She might find nothing, or she might find what happened to those twins, what happened to Cayley Drees, and what could happen to her if she did not stay alert and prepared. The shadow of the hawk announces its presence. Linda glanced up, hoping a shadow had not just passed over them.

25

SHERIFF MCBRIDE

JON MCBRIDE was uneasy. In his years with the Sheriff's Department he had never encountered something like this. There had been domestic disputes, including one that ended in a woman killing her husband in self-defense with a croquet mallet. There had been countless arrests for drunk driving, public intoxication, petty larceny and urinating in plain sight. But never the brutal murder of a young woman left twenty feet from her car on an isolated back road.

He'd been to the scene and could not shake the memories of what he'd witnessed there. What struck him most, besides the terrible tragedy of a life cut short, was that it seemed staged to him. He could not explain why, and he would have no verification of a sexual assault until the corner finished her report, but he had the distinct feeling that Cayley had been placed there after her death—that the location was in fact a body dump. But if this were true, where had she been killed? Had it been at the Cliff's Edge, in room #6? And wherever it had been, who had done it?

He didn't like Lenny Winfrow, but that was not enough reason to assume he was a murderer. It was not his job as Sheriff for Webley County to base his judgments on personal feelings or dislikes; if that were the case, quite a few people in Lonesome Pointe and the surrounding area would be guilty of something. He'd won election to office by a narrow margin, and he knew homophobia had played a part in his near-defeat. He harbored no ill will because of it. He knew almost everyone within a twenty mile radius and, despite not liking a significant number of them, he did not consider them especially prejudiced. Open gayness, while not new, was something to which people were still getting accustomed. Not only was Sheriff Jon McBride gay, but he was married to one of his deputies. As some residents would say, that made things a little more in-your-face. They had gotten used to it and regarded their sheriff as efficient and likeable, and would in all likelihood keep him on in the next election. But the respect had come grudgingly for some; he knew that and accepted it. He respected their boundaries and they respected his. He was paid to do a difficult job and he did it well, and in the end that's all that mattered to the mostly-good people who paid his salary.

Among those he did not like or trust, along with Lenny, were Meredith Vesey and Dolores Drover. He was sure—as were most in Lonesome Pointe—that the two women were more than old acquaintances who'd reconnected after Dolores came home. Vesey had been there all her life, but Drover had gone away and come back, by all accounts the prodigal daughter returned to make things right with her prickly father. McBride did not think it was a coincidence that Dolores inherited the motel. He guessed she knew her father was nearing his end. Maybe he'd written her letters talking of despair or a weariness with the world. Or maybe she had been the one to reach out. However it happened, the move had resulted in some degree of forgiveness and Russell had left the motel to her.

McBride made it his business to know what was going on in town, both the obvious and the gossip. He knew Dolores had started working at the motel a few months before her father's suicide. He knew she had taken a small apartment in town, and that she began spending more time with Meredith Vesey after Russell was dead. Had she avoided it while he was alive because he didn't like it?

"The Vesey bitch wants the place, but that ain't gonna happen."

He remembered those words, spoken in a short conversation with Drover a few weeks before his death. He'd stopped at the motel in response to a nuisance call from one of the guests. Another guest was drunk and shouting incoherently in the parking lot. By the time he got there the drunken man had passed out in his parked car, a bottle of Jim Beam on the seat next to him. Had the keys been in the ignition McBride would have arrested him for DUI, but they had not been. He had instead taken the keys from the man's pocket, laid him gently across the front seat, closed the door and pocketed the keys, telling Drover to let the man know he could retrieve his car keys at the Sheriff's Office when he sobered up.

That was when they'd had their chat. Drover had been alone that night. Lenny was off somewhere most likely doing something illegal, and Dolores had gone home for the night.

"She don't wanna live here, fine with me," Russell had said. "I offered her one of the rooms but she's got her pride, like her old man."

McBride had not wanted to stick around. The motel and its

owner made him uncomfortable. He knew Russell Drover was one of the people who didn't take well to a gay sheriff. But the night was slow and he believed it was better to make friends than enemies, so he let Russell talk.

"She'll be able to live here when I'm gone," Drover had said.

"You going somewhere, Russell?" McBride had asked.

"Same place we're all going, Sheriff. Most of us, anyway."

"I'm not a religious man," McBride said.

"Heaven's made for sinners," Russell continued, as if he had not heard or cared. Then, strangely, he said, "Hell's for people like Meredith Vesey."

McBride had not known there was any contention between Russell Drover and Meredith Vesey. It had not made its way into the loose talk he heard at Marge's Diner or in the shops in town.

"The Vesey bitch wants the place, but that ain't gonna happen."

More new information. Sheriff McBride knew the motel had been for sale, and that Russell had changed his mind about selling when his daughter came home.

"What do you have against Meredith Vesey?" he'd asked.

Drover had looked at him then, suspicion in his eyes. He knew when he was being pumped for information, and he was a man who did not provide it unless it served his purpose or he was paid for it.

"Never you mind that," Drover had said. He'd leaned back, away from the sheriff. It was his way of saying he'd spoken enough. "I'll be sure to tell Ralph you got his car keys, and not to come back here. I don't need drunks sleeping off their binges at my establishment. Got a reputation to maintain."

Yes, McBride had thought at the time, the Cliff's Edge could not afford to be known for what it was: a roadside dive where people ended up from desperation or a fall.

He'd left the motel, not thinking anything of the conversation until now. He had begun to think things; sometimes that led to the truth, and sometimes that led to false accusation. He was not yet ready to accuse anyone of anything, but he had a dead girl—for to him Cayley Drees was not much more than a girl—dropped at the side of the road like a bag of litter, who deserved the truth. Perhaps not justice, which was something Jon McBride put little stock in in a world with so little of it. But the truth.

He needed to pursue it. He needed to go from thinking things to knowing things, and he knew the place to start was the Cliff's Edge with Lenny Winfrow. He would not call ahead. He hoped Winfrow was back at the motel by now. Someone had to run the place, and he'd seen Dolores drive off earlier that afternoon. He would take his chances and drive back there. He wanted the element of surprise when he asked Lenny what really happened in room #6.

26

PLEASED TO MEET YOU

THE HOUSE was built to impress, that much was obvious to Linda as they pulled into the driveway. As she'd expected, she had not needed her GPS or even a street address: the Vesey house had its own road, Vesey Drive. She had not had time to research the town itself, but she assumed the Veseys were among the community's founders. How there came to be only one left, as Betsy had told them at the diner, was not her concern—if in fact that was true. Founding families tended to spread like tentacles; there were probably Vesey cousins and Vesey in-laws and Vesey descendants peppered throughout the surrounding county and even the state of Maine.

"It's a big house for one person," Kirsten said, staring up at the neo-colonial home Meredith Vesey lived in. It was Maine's idea of a mansion and, as such, it was impressive. Three stories, four if you counted the attic rooms that had windows looking out. "What happened to them all? The family, I mean."

"Well," said Linda, pulling up and parking behind two other cars, one a spotlessly clean Mercedes, "some things don't change much. Family lines still depend on males. If Meredith was an only child, and her parents and immediate relatives are dead or nonexistent, there's no one to continue the name."

"It's still too damn big," Kirsten replied. "Why would you have a house like this with just one child?"

"I think we'll never have an answer to that. Now excuse me, I need to take something out of the trunk, quickly and discreetly."

Kirsten knew she was talking about her gun. It was as much a keepsake as it was a reliable means of self-defense. Kirsten had watched Linda clean it countless times, and had even gone to the Horse Road Gun Club with Linda and watched her shoot—but only once. Guns were as foreign to Kirsten as rattlesnakes and she had expected never to encounter either one, until she met Linda.

"You go up and knock on the door, I need a little distraction," Linda said.

"What do I tell someone if they answer?"

"Tell them we'd like to talk to Meredith Vesey."

"About what?"

"About your book, try that. I'll be right behind you, but let's say you're writing a novel set in the area and the Vesey family is a big part of its history. You won't even get that much out before I'm there. Now go."

Kirsten did as she was told. She took a deep breath and climbed the front stairs that led onto an open porch. There were porch swings on each side and she suddenly had the desire to sit in one of them. She was imagining herself in a porch swing at Serenity House making notes for a second draft of her book when the door opened and a squat, homely woman smiled at her. She thought again of rattlesnakes.

* * *

Meredith and Dolores watched the women pull into the driveway. Meredith had just taken a call from Lenny upon his return to the Cliff's Edge. She told him she would speak with him later, they had unexpected company. She wasn't surprised they'd come here, but she had hoped they would not. She preferred having a plan, and she did not have one at the moment.

"Who are they?" Dolores asked, watching as one woman, the shorter of the two, got out and started up the walkway. The other one went to the trunk and was taking something out, but the car was angled and she could not see what the woman was doing.

"Snoops," Meredith said. "One's a retired detective, the other's her wife."

"Really?" Dolores said, her curiosity piqued. She dreamed of being Meredith's wife someday soon. She'd not dared to bring it up yet, but once the Cliff's Edge was in proper shape and they stopped keeping their open secret, there would be no reason not to marry.

"They mean us harm, Dolores," Meredith said. She knew what Dolores was thinking. She had no intention of marrying Dolores and would find a way to cause her a fatal accident long before the subject of matrimony could come up, but that was a plan for another day. Right now she had to think on her feet.

"You answer the door, Sweetie. I'll go in the back and come out like I hadn't heard the doorbell."

As it happened there was nothing to hear. Dolores opened the front door and smiled at the woman with her hand outstretched about to ring the bell.

"Good afternoon," Dolores said to Kirsten, noticing the look of surprise on the stranger's face. In it was a bit of fear, too.

"Hi. My name's Kirsten McClellan and I ..."

"We came to see if Meredith Vesey was home," Linda said, stepping up beside Kirsten. She kept her hand resting on her purse where she had slipped her pistol. "Might that be you?"

"Oh, heavens no," Dolores said. "I'm Dolores Drover, a friend of Meredith's."

"Don't be so shy," Meredith said, walking up next to Dolores and putting her arm around her. "We're more than friends now, Sweetie."

She kissed Dolores on the check, sending sparks and warmth flooding through her. She needed Dolores feeling secure, acknowledged and as bound to her as she could possibly be.

Linda was surprised at Meredith Vesey's openness. She knew it could only be because Meredith had identified them as a couple. She had mixed feelings about being treated with such familiarity by a woman they had never met.

"What can we help you with?" Meredith said.

"I'm writing a novel set in the area," Kirsten replied, "and the Vesey family is a big part of the town's history. I was just hoping for a few minutes of your time, to ask you some questions. I'm guessing you know as much about Lonesome Pointe as anyone who lives here."

"Oh, yes," said Meredith. "I know quite a bit. More than some people would like me to know, but that's life in a small town, isn't it? Please, come in."

She stepped aside, letting the women into her home. "We were just about to have some afternoon coffee. Would you like some? I'm happy to answer any questions you have, and there's no hurry. Please, join me in the living room."

She turned to Dolores and said, "Honey, would you make us some coffee? And that banana nut bread you made this morning, fresh and the very best."

"I'd love to," Dolores said, practicing speaking more like Meredith: refined, educated. She wanted to sound like that and had been mimicking the way Meredith spoke, at least when they were together.

Linda and Kirsten followed them into the house while Dolores disappeared down a hallway.

The living room was cavernous but comfortable in the way large old houses often were. There was a fireplace, two couches and an overstuffed chair. A plush white rug lay beneath a giant square coffee table that had fresh carnations in a vase sitting in its center.

Linda and Kirsten eased onto one of the couches. Linda let her purse strap slide from her shoulder, but kept the purse close. Something about their situation did not seem right to her and she was not going to let her gun be where she could not reach it.

"Now," Meredith said, sitting in the overstuffed chair facing them. "What did you want to ask me?"

27

THE CLIFF'S EDGE

LENNY HAD just arrived back at the Cliff's Edge when he saw the sheriff's car pull in. He was still sweating—mostly from nerves—after dumping Trevor Wilcox's body in the barn at the abandoned Garland farm. The property had never been for sale, even though there were no Garlands left in Lonesome Pointe or anywhere else as far as Lenny knew. Someone, somewhere, paid the taxes, had the "No Trespassing" signs replaced every few years after weather wore them out, and never set foot on the land. America was dotted with collapsed barns; the Garlands' (if, in fact, a Garland still owned it) was just another ghost house with a ghost barn made of rotted wood and faded paint. It wasn't completely true that no one went there; Lenny had spent quite a few nights in and around the barn getting high on an array of drugs and alcohol, as had most of the area's youth who were not inclined to the church life. But the body would be okay there for a day or three; by Monday it would be buried on the property, off in the woods somewhere. For now he just had to trust no curious trespassers would bother digging through the boards and planks under which Lenny had concealed a corpse.

"Morning, Sheriff," Lenny said, trying to calm his breathing and hoping he would not start perspiring again.

"Long past morning," McBride said, walking to the front desk, glancing around as if he were taking mental notes on the small room. "Mid-afternoon now, but nobody says, 'Good mid-afternoon,' do they?"

"I guess they don't. It's easy to lose track of the time on a busy day."

"I'm sure it is."

McBride stood no more than three feet from Lenny. He did not lean on the counter, but he might as well have. Lenny pulled back slightly, maintaining what distance he could between them.

"You been running a lot of errands today, Lenny?"

Lenny didn't like the sheriff. He had nothing against gay people, and from all accounts McBride was an exemplary sheriff, but that was the problem: gone were the days of being given a pass by a deputy whose sister was married to your cousin, or who would let you off with a warning because a small town connection made it the right thing to do. For Sheriff Jon McBride, the right thing was observing the laws as written, and favors were not asked for or extended. Lenny had spent time in the back of several deputies' cars and had been handcuffed in McBride's at least once. It had been a while, though, and Lenny hoped to keep it that way.

"Dolores keeps me busy," Lenny said. He was feeling calmer now; he knew he could pull this off. Just answer a few questions, smile, dip his head sheepishly a time or two, and get the sheriff on his way.

"So she told me," said McBride.

Lenny looked at him. He did not know McBride had been there when he was gone. Meredith hadn't told him.

"Sorry I missed her," Lenny said. "She was at the desk here? I put the sign up when I left, wasn't expecting to take so long."

"Actually she was busy cleaning one of your rooms."

"Really?" Lenny felt his pulse quicken again.

"Yes, really. Room number six. Said you folks had some unruly guests last week, pretty much trashed the place. That right?"

"That'd be a yes, Sheriff. Made a helluva mess. I'm embarrassed to say what we found in there."

"So no one stayed in that room last night?"

"That'd be a no."

"I'd like to take another look around in there," McBride said.

"You from the Motel Inspection Department?" Lenny said, immediately regretting his tone. He did not want the sheriff looking closely at room #6, or any other room.

"I don't mean to offend you, Lenny," said McBride. "I know you take real good care of this place. Russell trusted you, Dolores trusts you, must mean you're good at your job. I just want to take a look. Maybe those guests left something you missed. Might want to track them down and see if they'll pay for the cleanup. I'm guessing you don't have a record of who they were."

"No, Sir. We don't keep records here. Russell believed in discretion. And cash most times, let's be honest. But that's gonna change. The Cliff's Edge is gonna be a nice, proper motel when they get finished with her."

Jon McBride stared at him. "*They?*" he said. "Would that be Dolores Drover and Meredith Vesey?"

"Could be," Lenny said. "I mind my own business. All I know is Dolores has plans for the place, big plans, might even make me wear a name tag!" He fake-laughed, trying for a moment of comfortable familiarity.

The sheriff was not having it. "Let's just go take a look at that room," he said.

Lenny hopped off the stool. He glanced down at the 12-guage under the counter. It was visible from where he stood, but too big and too obvious: he couldn't very well walk the sheriff down to the room with a shotgun at his side. Besides, there was nothing to find, he was sure of it. If Dolores had cleaned the room, as McBride said, there would not be a single hair left behind. She was good at concealment, except when it came to her love affair with Meredith. That would be out in the open soon. The Drees murder would blow over, used as TV fodder on some cold-case show twenty years from now, and all would be right again. *But what if it isn't?* Lenny thought. What if the sheriff finds some reason for a warrant and has the room scanned with one of those lights that shows blood? There hadn't been any blood when he strangled the reporter. But maybe her nose bled, or maybe she'd trimmed her toenails last night and cut herself, leaving a drop on the bedspread. Things were going wrong, but it wasn't too late. He only had to keep playing his part a little while longer, then he could take the rest of the money Meredith promised him and get the hell away from here, far away.

"You head on to the room, Sheriff," Lenny said. "I'll be right behind you. Gotta get the master key."

McBride looked at him a moment. "Fine, Lenny," he said. "I'll see you at the room."

He left the office. Lenny knew he could not take long; the last thing he wanted was the sheriff coming back, wondering where he'd gone. He couldn't take the shotgun. He didn't have a handgun like Meredith's. But he did have a switchblade. They were illegal pretty much everywhere, and as popular as ever among knife enthusiasts. Lenny's was beautiful, with mother of pearl inlay on the handle, and had to date only been used to peel oranges and show his friends for effect. It might be time to put the blade to its proper use.

He opened one of two drawers in the cabinet below the cash

register. He kept the knife there, and felt himself getting sexually excited just looking at it. No woman could resist him with a switchblade in his hand. He had not yet used it for that purpose, although he'd had it in his pocket when he slipped into room #6 just past two-thirty a.m. that morning. If Cayley Drees had woken up she would have found a very thin, very sharp blade pressed against her neck. But she had not, and the blade had stayed in its sheath.

He took the knife, slipped it into his front pocket, and headed down to meet the sheriff. He glanced at the patrol car, calculating how quickly he could drive it around back and hide it under the carport. What he—*they*—would do from there was a decision to be made later. For now he hoped the sheriff would do his snooping, get it over with and be on his way. The switchblade and what he might have to do with it were a last resort, much like the Cliff's Edge itself..

28

MILK, NO SUGAR

LINDA REMAINED objective in most situations. She'd been an excellent police officer, then an exceptional homicide detective. Those were not appraisals she'd made of herself: her superiors had always held her and her performance in high regard. Her colleagues on the force had respected her, even if they hadn't always agreed with her. She had never been openly disliked; as for any private misgivings people may have had, she had not known about them and had not wanted to. It was this same professionalism she brought to the other areas of her life. She'd managed to make the little house in the woods her own—*their* own—and that had required detaching herself from sentimentality. Her aunt Celeste was gone. There'd been no reason to keep her belongings if they were better replaced by things Linda wanted to see in her home. And of course they had incorporated many of Kirsten's possessions—the artwork, the sculpture, the large desk Kirsten had brought from the real estate agency that no longer bore her name. Time only goes in one direction; that had been Linda's motto since the death of her father, and all the deaths that followed. Her own would come someday, too, there was no point in looking back. Stay calm, focused, clear, and always see what is ahead of you.

"Now, what did you want to ask me?" Meredith said, resting comfortably in her overstuffed chair, her arms draped on its armrests.

"You've been here all your life, I assume," Kirsten said.

"That would be a safe assumption, but still an assumption. I grew up in this house." Meredith waved her hand to indicate the entire structure around them. "I ran through this room, slid down that bannister. The unfortunate part was being an only child. There was no one chasing me except the housekeeper, and she was paid to play with me."

Linda did not get the feeling this was said for sympathy. Meredith struck her as someone whose isolation as a child had not bothered her.

"No cousins, no neighborhood kids?" Kirsten asked.

"The Vesey line was dying out when I was born. And look around when you leave. This house *is* the neighborhood. The nearest children were a mile away. I thought you were writing about the town?"

"Yes," Kirsten said, "I'm sorry, I don't mean to pry."

"It just seemed like a good place to start," Linda said. "Kirsten's novel involves an old, storied family in a small Maine town."

"It does," Kirsten said, letting Linda take it from there.

"It's a murder mystery, actually," Linda continued. "Small town secrets, a killing made to look like suicide ..."

"Really?"

"Yes. And an old, unsolved case."

"Well, you certainly picked the right town," Meredith said, smiling at Kirsten. "Your imagination's a little wild, but I suppose that's what makes mysteries popular. All that ... implausibility."

"Actually," Linda said, watching as Meredith turned the smile toward her, "Lonesome Pointe has quite an unsolved mystery of its own."

"Does it now?"

Linda leaned forward, her elbows on her knees. "Yes, it does. Something about two young boys disappearing, oh, forty years ago."

"I was fifteen years old then," Meredith said. "I remember it well. It was one of the first child abduction cases to go national. Missing children became all the rage after that."

"That's an interesting way to put it," Linda said.

"I only mean that was about the time it all started, kids on milk cartons and what have you. I don't remember the boys' names ..."

"Bradley. Todd and Christopher Bradley," said Linda. "Twins. Six years old at the time, I believe. Some people think there was a connection to the Cliff's Edge."

"You seem to know a lot already," Meredith said. Her smile was gone. "Why would you need me to tell you anything?"

"I thought you might have heard something or seen something, maybe something you didn't even realize was connected to the boys' disappearance."

"Had I seen anything or heard anything I would have told the police or my parents, now wouldn't I?"

"I just ... " Linda lowered her voice, glancing toward the hallway where Dolores had gone. "I thought perhaps Russell Drover, the owner of the Cliff's Edge …"

"I know who he was."

"… That maybe he had something to do with the boys being taken, or possibly knew who had done it."

"And you think I would have knowledge of this," Meredith said. It was not a question. "Maybe you think Russell Drover was killed all these years later to stop him from talking. Maybe he was planning to kill himself and wanted to get it off his chest before he died."

"No," Linda said, "I wasn't thinking that at all."

"It sounds like you were," said Meredith. "Your mystery involves a small town, a murder made to look like a suicide." And then, calling out, "Did you hear that, Dolores? They think a murder was made to look like a suicide. That sounds a lot like your father."

"Yes it does," Dolores said. Her voice startled Linda and Kirsten. They had not paid attention to where she had gone or what she was doing, assuming she would come back with coffee and a plate of banana nut bread. Instead she returned with a shotgun she was holding up, aimed directly at Linda. "It sounds like him because it was."

Seeing Linda reach toward her purse, Meredith said, "You can leave the purse where it is, Ms. Sikorsky. As a matter of fact, I'll take it. Just toss it on the floor this way."

Linda did as she was told, never taking her eyes off Dolores. She picked up her purse by the strap and gently flung it at Meredith Vesey's feet.

"I'm guessing there's a gun in there," Meredith said.

Linda's cell phone began vibrating inside the purse.

"And a phone, too!" said Meredith. "I think we'll let it go to voicemail."

Dolores slowly walked into the room, the shotgun still held up and aimed. Linda wondered if it was the shotgun used to end Russell Drover's life. And, of much more immediate concern, would it be used to end hers.

29

ROOM #6

SHERIFF MCBRIDE glanced around the room Lenny had just let him into. It looked exactly as it had when he'd been there earlier with Dolores. He wanted to make a closer examination now. He knew he would be prevented from this if Lenny simply insisted on a warrant, which the sheriff did not have and would not be able to obtain given the lack of any substantial justification. Imagined murders and the spiriting away of dead bodies did not impress a judge. Instead, he hoped that Lenny's natural inclination to do as he was told, especially when the person telling him had a badge and the power to make his life more difficult than it already was, would buy him enough time in the room to find something he could use as probable cause.

The room still smelled of bleach, and McBride noticed vacuum patterns in the carpet he had not paid attention to before. He made a mental note of it: find the vacuum cleaner. It could contain fiber and even DNA evidence. He was still not completely convinced anything had happened here, but Lenny and Dolores were not making it easier to dismiss what Linda Sikorsky had told him. Even if a transient couple had trashed the room a week ago, the timing of the clean up was suspicious. *Something* had happened at the Cliff's Edge and he was determined to find out what it was.

"You always clean the rooms like this?" he asked, walking slowly around the space, peering at the dresser, nightstand and bed—the missing bedspread and sheets had not been replaced since his earlier visit. The mattress looked as used as it was; he cringed at the thought of lying on it.

"Like what?" Lenny asked. He was behind the sheriff, standing by the door he had just closed, putting them alone in the room with the only way out tightly shut.

McBride paid no attention to the closing of the door. He wrinkled his nose. "All that bleach," he said.

"Kills germs," Lenny said. "And there was a lot of germs to kill, Sheriff. I knew that couple was trouble when they checked in."

"So how come you rented them the room?"

146

"We don't discriminate at the Cliff's Edge. Wouldn't be right."

"No," McBride said, "it wouldn't be. And I know you've got a reputation to maintain."

McBride headed into the bathroom. Lenny followed him, his hand slipping into his pants pocket for the security of the switchblade. He had not cleaned the room himself, and while he was confident Dolores had done an impeccable job of ridding it of any evidence, he could not be sure.

The sheriff and Lenny were in the small bathroom now. McBride walked to the shower and pulled back the curtain. The smell of bleach assaulted his senses. Dolores must have filled the bathtub with it. The tub itself was old and stained from minerals in the water—not something that could be scrubbed off with cleanser, but she had tried: only the natural stains from decades of running water were left to indicate the shower had ever been used. The chrome fixtures, as old as the tub itself, shone brightly. The tile had been scrubbed. The bathmat had been pulled up, then put back. McBride eased down on his haunches, reached into the bathtub and peeled the mat back.

Lenny was behind him now, not more than two feet, standing over the sheriff as he flipped the mat over and stared at it.

A single strand of long brown hair was woven between the suction cups. It could be recent, or it could have been clinging there for months.

Cayley Drees had long brown hair. McBride remembered it from staring at her body. He flashed back on the scene that morning by the roadside. A woman in her twenties, with her whole life ahead of her before it was abruptly stolen. She had been violated, exposed for any passerby to see, as well as the sheriff, the crime scene techs, and, soon enough, the coroner.

McBride reached into the tub, carefully pulling the strand of hair from the bottom of the mat.

"What's that?" Lenny asked. His voice was close, not far from the sheriff's ear.

McBride did not seem startled. He held the strand up with his left hand, staring at it.

"It's someone's hair, Lenny," he said. "Mind if I take this with me?"

"You'll need a warrant for that," Lenny said.

"I don't believe I do. You invited me in here, in a manner of speaking."

"Then I think it's time to invite you out," Lenny said.

The click of the switchblade sounded more loudly than Lenny expected it to in such a small space. He had not wanted this, not wanted it at all, but McBride had come where he wasn't welcome. He'd all but barged his way into other people's business. He had put Lenny into an untenable situation, forcing him to make a quick decision. A life-or-death decision, and Lenny chose death. There was no time to call Meredith, no time to ask her what to do. Ultimately, he knew she would tell him he'd done the right thing, there had been no other option. He stepped toward the sheriff who was still on his haunches, holding a strand of Cayley Drees's hair in his fingers.

He was about to bury the knife blade in the sheriff's neck when he felt his left leg yanked out from under him. How had he done that? Who was that fast? He fell backward, hitting his head on the bathroom door as he landed on his back.

Sheriff McBride, still squatting, leaned over Lenny with his service revolver aimed squarely at Lenny's chin. A bullet fired from it would enter below his jaw and exit through the top of his skull, taking most of his brain with it.

"Drop the knife, Lenny," McBride said.

Lenny did as he was told, opening his palm and letting the switchblade fall to the floor.

Lenny's calculation was quick and cold. He knew this would not go his way, but was there a bargain to be made? Maybe he could get himself into some witness protection program. Or maybe he could testify in court in exchange for ... *something*. He didn't know what, but he knew he had to try, quickly.

"I was only doing what she told me," Lenny said. "I didn't hurt nobody, I just helped her get rid of the body. I swear that's all."

McBride kept the gun on Lenny, reaching around with his free hand to take his handcuffs off his belt.

"Roll over," he said.

Lenny obeyed, turning over onto this stomach and putting his hands behind his back for the sheriff. He felt the handcuffs tighten, heard them close.

McBride stood up and yanked Lenny to his feet.

"Now who exactly told you to do something, and what did she

tell you to do? Are you talking about Dolores Drover?"

Lenny seemed offended at this. "Hell no," he said. "She's a loser, and dumb as a hammer. I'm talking about the boss, the one who pulls all the strings. Dolores couldn't pull a thread off a ratty towel."

"Meredith Vesey."

"That would be the one," Lenny said.

* * *

Ten minutes later Lenny was in the back of the sheriff's patrol car. The handcuffs cut into his wrists and he stayed sitting up, trying to keep pressure off them. He had been talking through the wire mesh that separated the front seat from the back.

"I let her into the room sometime around two, three o'clock this morning," he said. He had been telling a very altered story to McBride, making Meredith the killer as well as the mastermind.

"And then what?" said McBride. "You just watched her kill this young woman? Was she drugged first? Knocked out?"

"Didn't need it," Lenny said. "Too fast for that. Opened the door, let her slip in, and it was over in five minutes, tops. Then we moved the body. I'll admit to helping move the body, but I swear, Sheriff, I didn't know she was gonna kill her. I thought she just wanted to talk."

"At three in the morning."

"She's a strange woman, Meredith Vesey. Dangerous, too."

"What about Russell Drover?"

Lenny was surprised by the question. "What about him?"

"She kill him, too? She get you to help her make it look like a suicide?"

"It was a suicide, far as I know," Lenny said. He had not expected this and was not going to implicate himself in a second murder.

"You know what I think, Lenny? I think old Russell met his maker with a personal introduction, that's what I think."

"I didn't have nothing to do with that," Lenny said, as much as admitting the old man's death was not self-inflicted. "You might wanna talk to his daughter."

"I intend to," McBride said. They were just outside Lonesome

Pointe, where the sheriff planned to deposit Lenny Winfrow in a holding cell. "What else she make you do for her?" he asked.

"Follow those women around," Lenny said. "See where they went, what they got up to."

He left out the detail about strangling Trevor Wilcox and dumping his body at the Garland farm. He had a lot of thinking to do, maneuvers to make, but it was hard sitting in the back of a cop car with his hands cuffed behind his back.

"Are you talking about the women who came to see me? Linda Sikorsky and Kristen McClellan?"

"Those would be the ones."

"Where'd you follow them to?"

"Marge's Diner, the All Pointes office over in Wathingham."

"Where are they now?" McBride said.

Lenny did not respond. He had called Meredith when he got back to the Cliff's Edge to let her know he had disposed of Wilcox's body but would need help moving it as soon as they could. It would require another errand in the middle of the night. Meredith had told him she couldn't talk, they had unexpected company. He'd thought at the time, and was now all but certain, that company was the two women they were speaking of in the patrol car.

"I can't say for sure," Lenny said. "But I think they're at the Vesey house."

The information alarmed McBride. A woman he now believed was involved in at least two murders had the women in her home, where she would be most comfortable and could most easily harm them.

"Oh, shit!" McBride said. "Why didn't you tell me this sooner?"

"You didn't ask, Sheriff. What, you think they're in danger?"

"We're going to find that out."

"You wanna drop me off at the station first?" Lenny said, knowing it was pointless as he watched McBride make a sharp U-turn, heading up toward the house on the hill. They could see it in the distance. It had a way of *looming* over the town, and Lenny thought it would be a good day for everyone when the damned thing was torn down.

Sheriff Jon McBride pushed his accelerator, sending his patrol car barreling up the road. The force of it sent Lenny flying back in the seat, landing heavily on his own hands. The cuffs dug deeply into his flesh.

"Shit!" he said. "That hurt!"

McBride ignored him. He took out his wallet, opening it with his hands on the steering wheel. He found the business card Linda Sikorsky had given him. He held it between the fingers of his steering hand, then grabbed his cell phone with free hand and dialed.

Please answer, he thought, listening to Linda's phone ring, ring, ring. Finally it went to voicemail.

30

THE TWINS

JULY 4TH, 1976. The country was about to celebrate its 200th birthday. The nation's bicentennial had occupied the public consciousness for months. There was a sense of reverence for an event that would only happen once, as well as a sense of renewal: Jimmy Carter was running for president, promising to end the country's bleak extended period of disgrace and anxiety, and while economic times were challenging, people had hope.

The town of Lonesome Pointe was no different from thousands of towns in America. Celebrations were planned, including a rare fireworks display set to go off at sundown. This year people had stayed in town, wanting to be part of something historic. They didn't know what would happen, or exactly why it would be different from any other 4th of July celebration, but they knew it would be. They would remember this day for the rest of their lives, like where they'd been when JFK was shot (if they were old enough to have been anywhere), or how they'd felt seeing Neil Armstrong step onto the moon.

Meredith Vesey was doubly excited. Not only was Lonesome Point abuzz with anticipation for the most spectacular celebration in its history, but she was driving for the first time. She had gotten her learner's permit on Wednesday. It was now Sunday, and she had already taken her parents' car out twice by herself. This was against the law, which required she be supervised by an adult, but John and Sharon Vesey had gone to Seattle for a wedding and Meredith had no intention of waiting for them to return. It was not uncommon for them to leave her alone in the company of the housekeeper and the landscaper. She was fifteen and quite capable of looking after herself; she'd done it many times, beginning when she was just twelve. Before that there had been babysitters, and a nanny for several years in Meredith's youngest days. She was, by her own declaration, all grown up now and could be left alone for days at a time, weeks if need be.

She also had no concern for the law. She had been doing as she pleased all her life. Some would call her spoiled, and possibly neglected, but Meredith saw it as being independent. She stayed out past her 8:00 p.m. curfew if she felt like it, with no greater repercussion than a scolding. And if she felt like driving a few times, gambling that she would not be stopped (and confident in her abilities of persuasion if she were), so what? Her parents would be back on Monday, none the wiser that she'd tooled around the town and county in their Volvo.

Besides, she wasn't completely alone. She had Trevor Wilcox with her. Two years younger than Meredith, Trevor was what other kids called a loser, both behind his back and to his face. She had befriended him when they were in grade school some six years earlier, and it had proven to be a good decision. Trevor worshipped her, if only for a lack of any other gods to devote himself to. It was not a physical attraction; they'd been so young when they'd first met, especially Trevor, that sexuality played no part in it. And while it may have started as a crush for Trevor, it soon became devotion. Meredith was everything Trevor was not but hoped to be: outgoing, strong in will and presence, with a preternatural certainty to her own opinions and behavior that even few adults possessed. His fawning had allowed her, after a short probationary period, to share with him her darker passions, her behaviors anyone else would find appalling, if not criminal.

It began with stray cats. Meredith enjoyed poisoning them. She'd been only seven years old when she'd killed her first cat with a bowl of delicious pet treats mixed with mouse pellets. She'd been careful to remove the bowl as soon as the cat ate from it. She knew not to leave evidence. She had watched the cat over the next hour as it began to stumble. She followed it beyond her back yard, out among the trees where it went to die (cats were so smart about their own mortality), and she had watched with utter fascination as it vomited and convulsed its way to kitty heaven. From there it was only a matter of time and opportunity to her first dissection.

Cats proved too easy; and, as she decided at the time, when you've seen one cat die, you've seen them all. She graduated to dogs, choosing a distant neighbor's pet Pomeranians. By then she could ride her bicycle down the hill and take her pick, so long as she did some initial reconnaissance to be sure no one would see her. She'd had to take a break at one point, when an article appeared in the All Pointes Bulletin about someone poisoning local animals, with a follow up about them disappearing altogether. The dissections were both easier and trickier; she could do them alone in her parents' basement, unconcerned with being caught. Her timing on that matter was always impeccable. But she had to bury the carcasses, and that was best done with help. Enter Trevor Wilcox.

She welcomed but did not understand Trevor's devotion to her. He, too, was an only child, and she'd attributed some of his attachment to loneliness. She knew he had an absentee father who made long haul trips in various semi-trailers. His mother worked at the library reprimanding people for their late book returns. The Wilcoxes had been in Lonesome Pointe for several generations; it was common among the residents. Most people who lived here did so because they always had. It was not a place to which one moved for better opportunity or a finer lifestyle. Meredith first became aware of Trevor when she was in grammar school and saw him staring at her on the playground. It was a look of fascination, as if the taller girl was the most interesting creature he had ever seen. He still looked at her that way, and even when he found the things she did unpleasant, he would do as she said and had made himself increasingly complicit in her behavior.

Trevor had helped her bury animals in the woods. He'd even helped her flay a rabbit, stopping only to puke on the basement floor. Meredith had laughed at him and told him he had to clean up the rabbit entrails and the vomit. He meekly did.

On the day of the nation's biggest birthday celebration Meredith had picked up Trevor in front of his house. His father was gone again; he'd been gone so often Meredith wondered if he had run away. Trevor's mother was at some church function being a do-gooder, the role she alternated with library scold. It was just Meredith and Trevor, which was how Meredith preferred it.

Trevor had stared at the car with Meredith behind the wheel. He could not believe she had taken it, let alone driven over to pick him up.

"Aren't you supposed to have a grownup with you?" he'd asked through the passenger door when Meredith opened it for him.

"I'm the only grownup I know," she'd said, and laughed.

He'd climbed in and buckled his seatbelt, then stared in amazement out the window as Meredith took them on a joyride.

After driving around back roads for a half hour Meredith turned the car toward town. This, Trevor knew, was asking for trouble. People would see them, and some of those people worked for the sheriff. Others knew the Veseys and were sure to tell Meredith's parents they'd seen her driving their car when they were out of town.

"I think we should go back," Trevor had said, sitting up nervously and looking this way and that through the windshield.

"Don't be such a nervous nelly," Meredith had said. "I'll park a couple blocks off the main street, maybe in a lot. Nobody'll see us. Even if they do, what are they gonna say? I'll just tell them I got my driver's license and that'll be the end of that."

"But you're only fifteen," said Trevor.

"They don't know that, stupid! I could be seventeen, eighteen. I'm as old as I say I am. You worry too much."

She had then pulled into the bank parking lot, nearly empty on a Sunday, found a spot in the back and gotten out. Trevor followed.

"Where to now?" he'd asked, hurrying to catch up as Meredith headed out of the parking lot and onto the sidewalk.

"Let's go see what all the excitement's about," Meredith had said. She knew perfectly well what it was about: the country was getting ready for a massive party. The kind of noise, distraction and self-indulgence that made a perfect diversion from anything she might have in mind to do while everyone was preoccupied.

* * *

The Bradley twins were shopping with their mother. Their sister Rebecca had remained at home cleaning the house. They were expecting friends for dinner, the McAllisters and their two daughters, and all of them would be heading into town afterward for the fireworks.

Richard and Lisa Bradley were good parents by all accounts. Dickey, as most people called him, worked for the post office while Lisa raised their children at home. He was also a deacon at church, which is where he was on July 4th, 1976, helping paint the sanctuary. Lisa had asked him if they should all come help but he'd said no, the boys were too young to paint, and Rebecca could get the house ready for company. It had pleased Lisa to hear this, even though she pretended otherwise. They spent a good deal of time at church and she welcomed having a Sunday away from it. Her faith was as strong as her husband's, certainly, but she had three children to raise and a list of daily to-dos that sometimes went unmet when they were so often involved in church functions.

They were at Ludlow's General Store, then a thriving business that had been in town for forty years. It would not survive the 1980s, but in 1976 it was a going concern. There was a mechanical pony outside the store, as well as a wooden Indian and a gumball machine old man Ludlow or his son dragged inside every night when they closed up shop. Lisa had often let the boys play on the horse while she went inside. She would give them four or five dimes, which was what a mechanical animal accepted back then. She would do her shopping, come out and find them there, still taking turns riding the horse. That is what she had expected that Sunday. She'd had no reason to believe things would be different from any other day they'd gone there. She was wrong.

"Can I take a turn?" Meredith said.

Christopher was on the pony while Todd waited to use the next dime for himself.

Trevor stood back, wondering why a fifteen-year-old would want to ride a machine made for someone half her age.

Todd wondered the same thing. "You're too big," he'd said. "You'll break it."

Meredith had laughed, a lighthearted, girly trill that Trevor had not heard before and that he found ominous.

"Never mind," Meredith said. "I have a real horse to ride."

The pony stopped just then, needing another dime to keep it going. Christopher stared at her. He'd seen her around town but had never had reason to interact with her. She was much older and had not made any attempt to talk to them before.

"You do not," he said.

"Of course I do!" Meredith replied, laughing again. "We're rich. We have horses and dogs and cows. I even have my own giraffe."

With that, both boys' eyes widened. This was astonishing! Could it be true? How did someone get a giraffe, and what did they feed it? Did they use a ladder?

Trevor kept looking toward the door of the store, wondering where the twins' parents were.

"I don't believe you," Todd said as his brother climbed down off the pony. It was his turn to ride but he did not get on.

"I can show you," Meredith said, and Trevor felt a chill surge through him. He was only thirteen but he knew what Meredith was capable of. Maybe she only wanted to play with them. Maybe she just wanted to fool them, then laugh as she and Trevor walked away from the silly, gullible boys.

"We can't go anywhere," Christopher said. "Our mom's in the store."

"It's okay," Meredith had said. "I told her already. She said it was fine."

The boys looked at her, confused. It didn't make any sense that she had spoken to their mother when she had not come out of the store. Had she told her before they got there? Did she know their mother? They'd been instructed many times not to speak to strangers, but she was a kid, really. Kids aren't strangers. Men are strangers, maybe a woman who looked scary, but not a teenager.

"Come on," Meredith had said. "I'll show you and we'll be back by the time your mom comes out. I promise."

They twins looked at each other. Neither wanted to be the one to suggest they not go with this girl when they had the chance to see a real giraffe. And she said they would be back by the time their mother came out. How long could it take to see a giraffe? They'd be able to see it from a block away, with a neck that long!

"Okay," said Todd. "But we have to be back fast."

"Excellent," Meredith had said. "Let's hurry. I've got a car over at the bank parking lot, that'll get us there and back real quick."

The boys did not know where "there" was, but Trevor knew. His heart had fallen into his stomach, and his stomach into his feet. All the way back to the car he was sure he was going to be sick, but he had not been. It was only later, when he'd finally gotten home, that he had vomited two, three, four times, until he thought he was going to puke his entire insides out.

* * *

Trevor never knew if Meredith had intended to kill the boys. She'd said that was not the plan and that if they had simply promised to keep their mouths shut she would have taken them back to the general store. It was a disingenuous thing to say, considering she had never asked them to promise anything. Instead she had smiled as they cried for their mother. It was unimaginably cruel and the beginning of Trevor's disillusionment with Meredith Vesey. But he had come this far, witnessed this much, and said nothing about what he knew or what he had seen. He'd been as trapped as those twins, or at least that's what he had told himself. He could not tell anyone what had happened or what they had done. He was *part* of it. The part that watched as Meredith tied the boys up in her basement. The part that cringed but made no attempt to help as Meredith began poking and prodding them, as if they were dolls she wanted to make bleed. The part that made no real objection when Meredith had grown bored with them and strangled them, first Todd, then Christopher, troubled only by the stench of them defecating in their pants.

"Better than a cat," Meredith had said, staring at the small dead bodies tied to folding chairs beside the shelf of paint cans and household paraphernalia her father kept in the cellar. There were windows high on the walls, but no one to look into them up on the hill where the Veseys lived. No one to have heard the boys screaming, no one to rescue them.

Trevor had grown silent early on and had not said anything for twenty minutes. He'd stared at the small boys, now corpses, and marveled that he had not shit himself along with them.

"Well," Meredith had said, "we have to get rid of them now."

Neither of them knew of the commotion then taking place at the general store in town. They were unaware of the frantic searching, the calling out, the rising collective panic as Lisa Bradley and a dozen townspeople went searching for the boys who had vanished—just vanished!—as if into thin air.

"What do you mean?" Trevor had said, finally willing himself to speak.

"Umm, they're dead," said Meredith. "I can't just leave them here, stupid."

It was the first time he'd realized she often called him "stupid."

"What do you want to do?" he's asked.

"Bury them, of course," she'd said, as if it were the most obvious response she could offer.

The sun was still out; it was only mid-afternoon.

"Somebody could see you," Trevor had said.

"Not *now* .." she'd said, then hesitated, as if she'd been about to call him stupid again but thought better of it.

"We'll wait till it's dark. You can stay out, can't you?"

It was not a question, but an expectation. Trevor would not be going anywhere until they had seen this through to its ugly end.

And that is how the Bradley twins, Todd and Christopher, aged six with only two minutes separating them at birth, came to be buried in the woods behind the Cliff's Edge. Meredith knew the land well. She knew the motel, too, and how those who went there were busy looking the other way.

Meredith and Trevor drove just after sunset to the small dirt side road that ran perpendicular to the property. Sometimes the town's teenagers parked there to have sex, but that night they had the road to themselves. It was the nation's bicentennial, after all, people were in town to watch the fireworks or already too drunk to notice anything. Meredith was not surprised; she was lucky that way. She parked the Volvo and in very short order had Trevor help her get the bodies into the woods, where they were buried as deeply as Meredith and Trevor could dig, then covered up with dirt and hidden with surprising effectiveness beneath branches and leaves. The brush there was thick; it was not a place anyone came to drink beer or have sex. It was, as the years proved, the perfect place to bury children.

Meredith had put the shovel back in the trunk and closed it, wiping her hands on her jeans. She'd seen the disgust on Trevor's face, something he never forgot, then laughed at him and got into the car.

"I'm hungry," she'd said, driving back into town. "You want a milkshake?"

Trevor had not wanted anything to eat ever again. He had done something terrible, something that would have him leaving town and doing his best to disappear as completely as the boys had. Something that would, twenty years later, get him killed and buried with even less concern.

31

PUSH COMES TO SHOVE

LINDA KEPT as calm as she could with a shotgun aimed at her and her only means of defense, her gun, tucked at the bottom of a purse Meredith Vesey was now rummaging through. Watching Meredith pick through her belongings felt like more of a violation than having Dolores pointing a 12-guage at her that could send a thousand shotgun pellets blasting through her chest with the yank of a trigger.

"I read about you, you know," Meredith said. She'd pulled out a package of Kleenex, examined it as if it might hide a listening device, then dropped it back in Linda's purse. "You have quite a history with killers."

Linda remained silent. She was keenly aware that Kirsten was also saying nothing as she sat next to Linda on the couch, glancing nervously back and forth between Meredith in her chair and Dolores just inside the doorway. Knowing Kirsten trusted her to somehow protect them made her all the more determined to find a way out of this.

"You don't want to talk about it?" Meredith prodded.

"It's not something I'm proud of," Linda replied. And it was true: she had stopped several high profile killers, all with the help of her friend Kyle Callahan (*note to self*, she thought, *live long enough to tell Kyle about this one*), but catching, or even killing, serial murderers was something done of necessity, for justice and to prevent more harm, but not to take pride in.

"I think I'd have their heads mounted on my wall," Meredith said, smiling.

"She would, too!" Dolores had not spoken for several minutes. She'd stood fewer than ten feet from them, holding the shotgun up, ready to send them both flying backward against the couch they sat on.

"Ah, there it is," Meredith said.

She pulled out Linda's gun. It sent a wave of anger flooding through Linda. This was not just her gun, but *her father's gun*. The one he'd had with him as Military Police in Vietnam. The one he insisted he had never fired, at least not at another human being. The one Linda had cherished, cleaned and cared for since her mother gave it to her upon her graduation from the Police Academy. And here it was being handled by a woman as violent, vile and dangerous as anyone Linda had ever met. A woman responsible for at least two deaths—those of Russell Drover and Cayley Drees—and possibly more for which she had never been held accountable.

"They don't make 'em like that anymore," Meredith said, examining the gun. It was a Colt .45 series government model, very different from the firearms used by police today. It wasn't exactly an antique—it was still lethal and still very much in working order—but its real value was sentimental. The more Linda watched Meredith handle the gun, the more furious she became.

"Have you killed anyone with it?" Meredith said, sliding the gun back into Linda's purse.

"Not yet," Linda said, smiling.

Meredith liked that. She smiled back.

"What are we gonna do with them?" Dolores asked. She was standing stock still just inside the room, holding the shotgun casually now. Its barrel had slid downward, pointing more at the floor than at the women, but Linda did not doubt Dolores would swing it up in an instant and shoot them both if she thought she had to.

"I'm thinking about that," Meredith said. She set Linda's purse down on the chair beside her. "How about we move to the basement. That's a start."

And a finish, thought Linda, her sense of self-preservation now on high alert. It was in a basement on Manhattan's Upper East Side where her life had nearly ended at the hands of the Pride Killer. A cool, refinished cellar that had almost been her tomb—as it already had been for the men Diedrich Keller had murdered. She did not intend to enter Meredith's basement, and she had to think quickly now how to prevent it.

* * *

Lenny cursed himself for saying anything to the sheriff about the women's whereabouts. He was not certain they were at Meredith's house; fairly sure of it, but not something he could swear to—or admit to in court, if it came to that. He'd been thinking all the time he was in the backseat of the patrol car how to finesse a bad situation getting worse. After all, he wondered, what could he actually be connected to with hard evidence? If he was accused of filling Russell Drover full of shotgun pellets, he could easily say it had been Dolores who'd pulled the trigger. If he was somehow connected to the murder of Cayley Drees, he could say it had been Meredith who had killed her, that he'd given her the key to room #6 and merely helped dispose of the body, that's all. There was always a way out, he just had to find it.

"Sheriff McBride," Lenny called out, sitting up as best he could on the edge of the backseat.

"Shut up, Lenny," McBride shouted back, focused on his driving as he sped up the hill toward the Vesey house.

"I want to make a deal!"

"You already did … with the Devil. Whatever arrangements you made with him, you have to talk to him about, not me."

Lenny could see the house in the distance. They were getting there fast; he knew he only had minutes to spare before they would fly up the driveway.

"She's got a gun," Lenny said, hoping it would at least get the sheriff to listen to him. He could play the good guy, the helper of authority.

"I'd expect that," McBride said. "I've got one, too. Now shut up and sit back, this isn't about you anymore, not yet. We'll get to that later."

"I know things," Lenny said, trying a last time to influence the man who might be able to help him in any delicate negotiations held with a district attorney. *Oh, Lenny Winfrow, he was very cooperative. Lenny Winfrow warned me about Meredith Vesey having a gun. I honestly don't think Lenny killed anyone* … "I know who killed Russell and Cayley. She wanted the property. She don't give a damn about Dolores, I'm sure of that, Sheriff. Meredith wanted that motel and she got it."

McBride thought a moment, listening to Lenny for the first time as he maneuvered around a curve. They were no more than a minute or two from the house.

"How come she wanted it? What's so special about that piece of crap motel?"

Lenny leaned up, getting as close to the mesh divider as he could.

"There's treasure there," he said. "Somewhere in the woods out back. Old Russell Drover buried a lot of money, that's what I think. Never trusted banks with his cash, he had to hide it somewhere. He was gonna sell the place, dig up his booty and get the hell out of Dodge. Meredith and Dolores got to him first."

It was an intriguing idea but one that made no sense to McBride. Why kill a man for something he'd buried himself and could easily unbury any time he wanted to? If, however, there was something buried on the property Russell Drover did *not* know about ... but what could that be?

He set aside thoughts of the Cliff's Edge and whatever fatal secrets it held as he roared into the Vesey driveway. He saw three cars parked in front and guessed one of them belonged to Linda and Kirsten. He turned right into the driveway and sped up the incline, coming to a halt not six feet from the steps.

"You wait here," McBride said, leaping out of the patrol car. Lenny didn't have a choice, being locked inside. McBride thought in that moment he should have called for backup, but it was too late now. He was at the house, heading for the steps, reaching back and taking his gun off safety. Something wasn't right here, he could feel it. Call it instinct, call it gut reaction, it was the kind of thing that saved a cop's life and for some reason, as he climbed the stairs to the front door, he thought his life just might need saving.

* * *

"It's a busy day for company," Dolores said. She had a view out the front window and saw the sheriff rushing up the walkway.

"Step back!" Meredith barked. "Before he sees you."

Dolores did as she was told, quickly moving backward through the doorway but keeping the gun pointed at Linda.

Meredith was not someone to panic, but she was doing it now. She felt her mind racing as she tried to decide very quickly what to do.

"Listen," she said to Linda and Kirsten. "Keep your mouths shut. I'll let him in, say a few things and get him out of here. If he asks you if you're okay, the answer is yes. If the answer is anything other than yes, Dolores steps back into the room and blows a hole through one of you. She can take her pick, I don't care. Is that understood?"

Linda and Kirsten nodded.

"I don't hear you."

"Yes," Linda said, calmly but loudly.

"You hear all that?" Meredith said, aiming her words at Dolores, who she could not see beyond the doorway.

"Got it!" Dolores called back.

An insistent knock came at the door.

Meredith hesitated, took a deep breath. She walked to the front door.

Linda looked over at her purse on the chair Meredith had gotten up from. The gun was there. But so was Dolores, standing just out of everyone's line of vision, with the shotgun ready to unload at the first provocation. Could Dolores see her, too? Would she know if Linda leapt for her purse?

"Good afternoon, Sheriff McBride," Meredith said, standing in the doorway to block his entrance. "What a nice surprise."

McBride knew instantly something was wrong. There was fear in the air and he'd had a nose for it from the first moment he'd put on a uniform. Each of the senses was crucial in his line of work, and each had been honed over his years with the Department. His survival could depend on it.

"Afternoon, Meredith," he said, standing in the doorway. "Mind if I come in?"

"Not at all." Meredith stepped aside. She trusted that Dolores, listening from beyond the doorway, would move slightly back if she thought McBride was getting to a position where he could see her.

McBride entered the house, glancing around as he stepped inside. He scanned the room, looking quickly for anything amiss. What he saw was Linda and Kirsten sitting on the couch, facing away from him.

"Hello, Sheriff McBride," Linda said over her shoulder, not turning around.

"Afternoon, Ms. Sikorsky. Everything all right here?"

Meredith closed the door behind McBride as he walked into the living room. "Everything's fine, Sheriff," she said. "We were just getting to know each other. Did you know Kirsten here is a writer?"

"Can't say I did."

"Yes, and she's writing a book about our little town."

"Not about Lonesome Pointe specifically," Kirsten said. The composure in her voice surprised Linda and gave her hope; they would need to be as grounded now as possible.

"That's right," said Meredith. "You writers have to fictionalize everything, avoid lawsuits and what have you." Then, to McBride, "Is there something I can help you with, Sheriff? I'm sure you're busy and want to be on your way."

McBride looked around again. "Where's Dolores?"

"She doesn't live here," Meredith said. "In case you didn't know."

"Isn't that her car outside?"

Meredith's feigned smile slid from her face. "Yes it is, but she walked into town on an errand for me. She needs the exercise. We all do at our age, even you, Jon McBride."

Linda could sense things taking a wrong turn, tension slowly creeping into the air. "Excuse me," she said, sitting up. "Would you mind handing me my purse, please?"

McBride turned and looked at Linda's purse in the chair.

Meredith quickly moved into the room. "I'll get it for you," she said, hurrying to grab the purse while McBride was still confused.

He leaned down and took Linda's purse by the strap. "It's okay, I've got it."

"It's not okay," Meredith said darkly. "It's not okay at all."

"Drop the purse, Sheriff."

McBride was startled by the sound of Dolores's voice. Still holding Linda's purse, he turned around and saw Russell Drover's daughter standing in the doorway, aiming a shotgun at him.

"I said drop the purse," Dolores repeated. Then, to Meredith, "Take his gun."

Meredith hesitated only a moment. Things had gone quickly and completely wrong. If there was any way out, it did not include letting the three people in her living room leave her house. Could she lock them in the basement and flee? How difficult and complicated would it be to kill them and ... then what? The landscape had become littered with bodies. She didn't think they could dispose of many more and still escape. She approached the sheriff carefully from behind, removed his service pistol and held it to her side.

McBride let Linda's purse fall to the floor. From the sound of its *thunk* on the floorboards he guessed there was something heavy in it, probably a gun.

"We were talking about the town's history," Linda said. She could tell by their expressions it threw them off: they were in imminent danger, and she was talking about Lonesome Pointe. She watched as Meredith glanced back at her, Dolores glanced at Meredith, and McBride stood perfectly still.

"Were you aware, for instance, Sheriff," Linda said, "that Meredith knows what happened to those twins who disappeared?"

It was a calculated guess. Linda had no idea what Meredith knew or did not know, but she had to take the chance, she had to keep things moving while she and McBride waited for an opening, a chance to strike.

"The Bradley boys?" Dolores asked. "Nobody ever found them. Someone took those children out of town, out of the state. They're all grown up now."

"That's a nice scenario," said Linda. "Wanting them to still be alive after all this time. But they're not, Dolores. They've been dead for forty years and Meredith knows what happened to them, don't you?"

"What's she talking about?" Dolores said, staring at Meredith while still pointing the shotgun at McBride.

"I don't have any idea," said Meredith, "and neither does she. She's trying to distract you, Sweetheart, don't fall for it."

Linda could hear just a bit of worry seep into Meredith's tone. It occurred to her then: Meredith *did* know what happened to the boys, but Dolores did not. Whatever information Meredith had, she had kept from her precious puppet … the one with the shotgun and a fondness for using it. *Had Dolores killed her own father?* she wondered. Anything seemed possible at this point.

"Is that why all this happened? Why you killed your father?" Linda asked, sitting up on the edge of the couch. She signaled with the slightest wave of her hand for Kirsten to remain silent and let this play out carefully, cautiously. Linda would take the risks, Linda would play with fire.

"Nothing happened," said Dolores. "My father killed himself. He left the Cliff's Edge to me. That's all, there's nothing more to it."

"But there is," said Linda. "There's a dead young reporter, at the very least. Maybe a dead informant, too, since it seems clear Cayley Drees went to the Cliff's Edge to meet someone."

"She won't be talking to anyone again, nosy bitch," Dolores snorted.

"Shut up!" snapped Meredith.

"What won't she be talking about?" Linda said. "What was the story Cayley was here to find out? Was it that *you* knew what happened to the boys, Dolores? Maybe Meredith wasn't the one with the secret after all. Maybe it was you. You knew your father took those twins and ... killed them? Did you see it happen?"

"Lies!" Dolores screamed. "My daddy was a bastard, that's for damn sure, but he wasn't a killer, a *pedophile*."

"So who was the killer?" Linda said. And then it hit her, then she knew. She looked at Meredith and said, "It was you, wasn't it?"

"That's insane," Meredith said. She turned to Dolores and commanded, "Shoot her! Shoot them all!"

"I get it now," said Linda. "At least I think I do. That's why you've pretended to love this woman, isn't it?"

"I haven't pretended to love Dolores. It's very real, so real we'll be leaving this town together, very soon."

Dolores looked at Meredith, confused. "Leaving town? But I thought ... our beautiful hotel ..."

"Do you believe her?" Linda said to Dolores. "Do you believe she wants you, here or anywhere else? Or did she just want the Cliff's Edge?"

McBride saw his chance and spoke up. "It's not money buried there, is it? Lenny said he thought it was treasure old Russell stuck in the ground. But it wasn't Russell, and it wasn't cash. It was bodies."

"Shut up!" Dolores shouted. She raised the shotgun, aimed squarely at Sheriff McBride's chest. But instead of pulling the trigger and cutting him in half with shotgun pellets, she stopped.

"Shoot him!" Meredith cried again.

"I remember those boys," Dolores said, her voice low and quiet. "I remember you, too, Meredith. You and Trevor playing in the woods behind the motel. I wasn't even twelve years old then. Just a kid."

"What are you waiting for, Sweetie?" Meredith's voice was strained, her use of the word "Sweetie" sounding as false as it had always really been.

"Kids don't kill kids," Dolores said, in a way that made it sound rhetorical: somehow, on some level, she knew now what had happened, or at least she imagined it well enough to lock the puzzle pieces into place. Meredith and Trevor, or perhaps just Meredith, had harmed those boys. Maybe she hadn't meant to kill them, but they had died. Then she and Trevor had done something with them ... something at the Cliff's Edge. It all made sense now, horrible, shameful sense. Meredith wanted the property to make sure no one else would get it and find what she'd hidden there all those years ago ... *who* she had hidden there.

"You're a monster," Dolores said. She slowly turned, the shotgun barrel arcing in the air as she swung it from McBride to Meredith.

The explosion was deafening in the house, the sound of the gun firing with a *bang* that bounced from wall to wall.

Shocked, Dolores looked down at her own chest, where Meredith had just put a large bullet hole from the sheriff's gun. She appeared to speak, perhaps to ask why the love of her life had just shot her, when she fell forward onto the floor, the shotgun clattering and sliding away.

That was when Linda made her move. She flew from the couch, grasping at Meredith's arm that held the gun she'd just used to kill Dolores. Meredith was quick and stepped away, but not before Linda tackled her, sending them both to the floor, wrestling for control of the pistol.

Kirsten had leapt up but did not know what to do. She couldn't entangle herself with the women on the floor, one of whom was her wife. Instead she stared in horror and hope as Linda managed to keep Meredith's arm pinned in a way that prevented her from aiming the gun.

Linda, sensing she had the upper hand but not confident, suddenly saw the shotgun barrel enter her field of vision.

"Drop the gun," McBride said. Without hesitation, he placed the double barrel just inches away from Meredith Vesey's face. "Don't think I won't pull the trigger."

Meredith had no doubt he would. Of all the ways she had imagined her life ending, having her head blown off on her living room floor was not one of them. She loosened her grip on the gun and let it fall from her hand.

Linda quickly sat up, grabbed McBride's gun and stepped away. She kept the pistol down, not using it to confront Meredith, not involving herself in any way. This was up to McBride.

With Meredith still lying on the floor, refusing to even sit up for fear the sheriff would shoot her, McBride reached for his radio and called the dispatcher.

"Gerry," he said into the handset when he got a response, "we have a situation here."

32

SERENITY HOUSE

WE HAVE a situation here. Those five words had echoed in Linda's mind for the past fourteen hours. She heard them now as she stared toward the beach from their second floor balcony. Serenity House was all Kirsten had promised it would be—serene, beautiful and, after everything that had happened, very needed.

They'd spent much of the previous afternoon and evening sitting in a room at the Sheriff's Department describing what happened, over and over. Sheriff McBride had his own version of events, which differed only slightly from Linda and Kirsten's telling—a word here and there, a gesture. They had all been in the same room, witnessed the same things. Dolores had been unaware that Meredith had killed the twins when she was just a teenager and they were mere boys, an unspeakable act only Trevor Wilcox had known about because he was there. (Where Trevor was now remained undetermined; Meredith had summoned her attorney just before refusing to speak, and Lenny Winfrow wouldn't talk until he had a deal, which he insisted must include immunity from all prosecution and to which the District Attorney responded with derisive laughter.) Just as Dolores was deciding to shoot Meredith instead of any of them, Meredith got the upper, faster, hand and put a bullet from McBride's gun squarely and lethally into Dolores's chest. Then it had been a blur as Linda made a move for the gun, and McBride managed to grab the shotgun in time to stop another killing, pressing it against Meredith's face with terrifying finality.

So many more details had to be sought and revealed, details Linda and Kirsten would not know about for days and weeks to come. Among those details: how many others had Meredith Vesey killed? Monsters of her nature rarely stopped. She may never admit to more, and the world may never know, but Linda suspected there were bones out there waiting to be collected if the story were to truly have an ending. And while Linda was most curious to find out everything she could, personally and professionally (for even she knew that *Detective Linda* would always be key to who she was),

Kirsten was ready to put it behind them as quickly as possible. Her first-hand involvement with murder and the people who commit it had shaken her, at least temporarily. She confessed to Linda on the drive to Cape Haven that writing about killers was a far cry from encountering them, and that she hoped to never be closer to another one than the keys on her laptop. Imagining them would suffice for her.

Linda could hear movement on the balcony next to theirs. Another lesbian couple they'd met as they checked in just after the kitchen closed. Dianne and Rue were their names, Dianne the older of the two. The women had just finished eating in the house's small dining room. Serenity House, unlike most bed and breakfasts, offered a limited dinner menu. Linda and Kirsten had hoped to make it in time to try the food, but they'd been delayed by several murders and the need to give lengthy, repetitive statements to the authorities. As they checked in, Dianne and Rue were headed to their rooms and stopped to introduce themselves. Now Linda could hear one of them milling about on the adjacent balcony. She did not want to be nosy, or, for that matter, interrupt her own enjoyment of the morning's silence.

She looked forward to exploring Cape Haven while Kirsten sat on this very balcony finishing her first Rox Harmony mystery. She wondered if any of the events of the last two days would somehow make it into a second draft, or possibly the next book. She believed in Kirsten partly because she wanted Kirsten to believe in herself. She wasn't much of a reader, but she'd resolved to become one, at least of her wife's novels.

"Hey, why so early?"

Linda turned to see Kirsten standing in the doorway that led from their suite onto the balcony. Yes, a suite, one of only two offered by Serenity House. Linda had insisted on the upgrade when they checked in, and on paying for it. Few debut novelists could afford suites. Even though Kirsten, retired from her own very successful business, had more money than Linda ever would, she was a writer now, and writers lived on budgets, at least until they sold the movie rights.

Silly dreams, Linda thought, looking at her lovely wife silhouetted in the morning light. It wasn't long ago that the life she had now was just a dream, something she had not imagined for herself because she dared not. A peaceful, full existence in a small house with deer in the yard; a woman she knew, just *knew*, she would grow old with. The rest, as her late father Pete would say, is gravy.

"I wanted to see the sunrise," Linda said. "And you, standing in the doorway. You ready for some coffee?"

"I'd love some," Kirsten replied, stepping out onto the balcony. "And then I want to run some ideas by you."

"For the book."

"Yes, for the book," Kirsten said.

She took a seat next to Linda as Linda got up, about to head into the room to brew their coffee. "I think we're going to like it here, Detective."

Linda stopped in the doorway. She stared at Kirsten, her heart filling with something beyond love, whatever that something might be. Something vast, powerful and reassuring. And while she hoped this was not the beginning of Kirsten calling her "Detective", she didn't really care. Everything she cared about was sitting in a chair, on the balcony of a room at Serenity House, waiting for her to make the coffee.

NEXT UP

Horse Road Gun Club Blues: A Detective Linda Mystery

In Book 2 of the Detective Linda Mysteries, Linda finally gets Kirsten to take up shooting in a serious way. Linda's comfort with guns is lifelong and well known; among her most prized possessions is her late father's Vietnam War-era service pistol, which she lovingly maintains and regularly takes to the local shooting range on Horse Road, just a short distance from their house in the woods. The Horse Road Gun Club members are good people, as Linda calls them, and they had invited Linda and Kirsten to join the Club within weeks of the women moving into the community. Linda immediately took them up on it, while Kirsten had to think about it for awhile

After a year of gentle prodding, Linda coaxes Kirsten to the gun club for a membership and lessons in the proper use, care and treatment of firearms. There's just one problem: someone killed the owner of the club the night before they showed up. Was it jealousy? Was it love gone bad? Or was it property, given the gun club's fondness for expansion into its neighbors' lands, acquiring them by hook and, some say, by crook. Linda and Kirsten find themselves entangled in their rural neighbors' love-hate history ... a history filled with dark corners and drenched in blood and greed.

The Marshall James Mysteries: Murder at the Paisley Parrot

Welcome to the world of Marshall James. Marshall is a 57-year-old New Yorker with a knack for survival: he's outlived seven cats, two aquariums, a grave early prognosis for lung cancer, and most of the friends he had from his years as a bartender in Los Angeles ... long ago and not so far away. For the stories Marshall has to tell are only as distant as his memories. The doctors gave him three months to live when they found two spots on his left lung. Nasty spots that might as well have been craters blown into his soul by a vicious God who thought killing someone as durable as Marshall would be good for a laugh. Three years later Marshall is still alive, minus the lung, and God is still waiting for the punchline.

Marshall decides the time has come to tell a story or two. Stories about those murders in Hollywood back in the mid-1980s, when Marshall was pouring bourbon and gin into the glasses of men who didn't know they were dying, and he ended most nights with a handsome stranger in his bed—sometimes the same handsome stranger who ordered a double vodka rocks six months later looking pale, thin and terminal.

The Marshall James Mysteries begin with *Murder at the Paisley Parrot*. Every town has its dive bars, and Hollywood in 1985 had more than most. Bottom of the list was the *Paisley Parrot*, located just a half block from corner of Sleaze and Decrepit. The kind of bar where drunks felt at home, slurring their speech into sticky glasses while a cigarette burned their fingers. Marshall James's favorite kind of bar, and the bar he was working at when the murders happened. What murders, you ask? Here, let him tell you … in *Murder at the Paisley Parrot*, coming to a barstool near you in 2017.

A NOTE FROM MARK

Thank you for taking a ride on the mystery train, I hope you've enjoyed the scenery and the company. If you have a moment to write a review that would be much appreciated. Even a few sentences helps other readers discover the books and meet the characters.

You can find me at my website, MarkMcNease.com, and also on Twitter, Facebook and Goodreads. I'm always happy to hear directly from readers as well, and I answer every email, so don't be shy, drop me a note anytime at mark@markmcnease.com.

Writing is both my passion and my pleasure, and by the time you read this I'll be working on the next story … and the next.

Yours from the thickening plot,

Mark